SQUIRREL ISLAND

Published by the Larks Press
Ordnance Farmhouse, Guist Bottom,
Dereham, Norfolk NR20 5PF

01328 829207

Printed by the Lanceni Press
Garrood Drive, Fakenham, Norfolk

OCTOBER 1998

British Library Cataloguing-in-Publication Data
A catalogue record for this book is available from the British Library

ISBN 0 948400 75 7

SQUIRREL ISLAND

by

Jane Finch

Illustrations by Frank Thomas

The night is darkening round me,
The wild winds coldly blow,
But a tyrant spell has bound me,
And I cannot, cannot go.

The giant trees are bending
Their bare boughs weighed with snow,
And the storm is fast descending,
And yet I cannot go.

Clouds beyond clouds above me,
Wastes beyond wastes below,
But nothing drear can move me,
I will not, cannot go.

Emily Bronte

The Larks Press

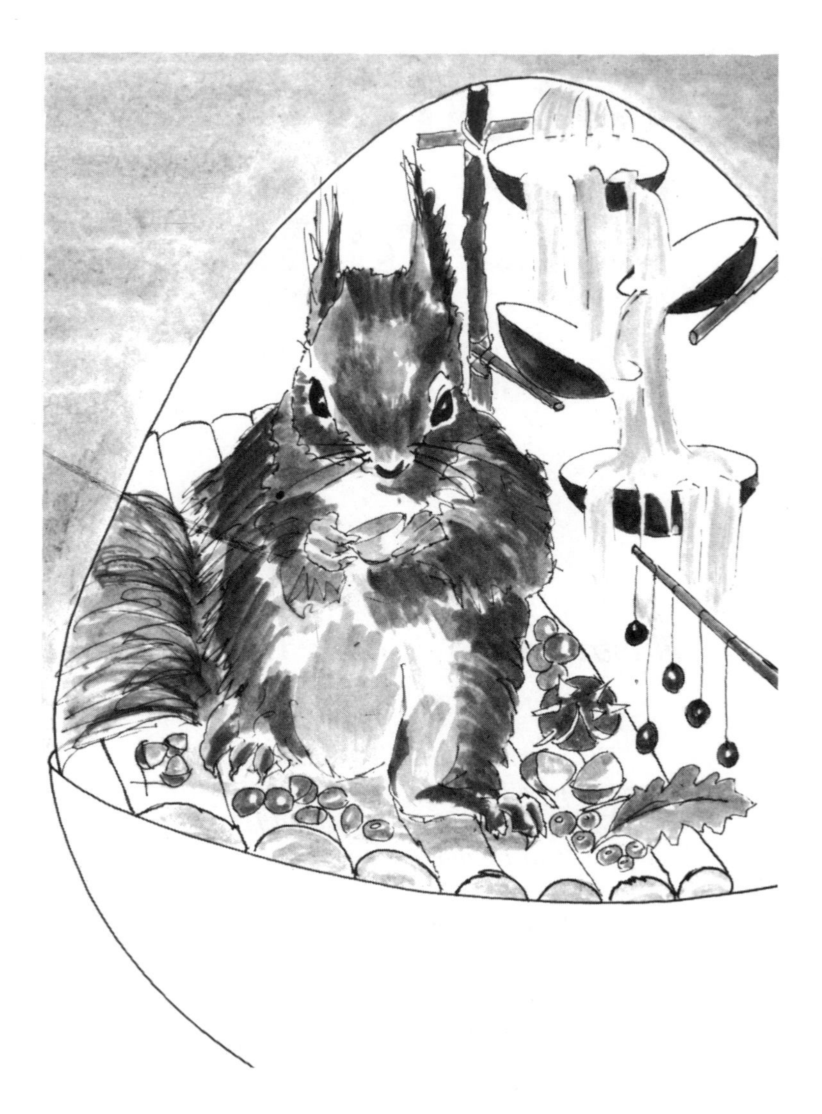

A magnificent feast

CHAPTER ONE

The acorn was the largest that had ever been seen before. It towered over the whole hill, rising high up into the clouds. A squirrel could run and run until he was out of breath and still not be able to see beyond the giant. The shell, crisp and hard, was so shiny that it reflected all around it. The female squirrels would sit before it admiring themselves, endlessly preening their magnificent tails and whiskers.

Right at the bottom of the massive acorn, just visible, stood a tiny door; there was no handle. But as a squirrel approached it opened magically on its own, revealing the splendours within. Only a glimpse, and then the squirrel entered, and the door closed again.

Rowan was mesmerised. Quickly he ran to the door. It opened as before and he hurried inside. Before him lay a magnificent feast. Long lines of tables piled high with pine cones, fresh young chestnut leaves, and dark, succulent fruits. The floor was covered with yew, juniper, oak, beech and birch leaves. In the centre of the drey (for what else would it be?) was an enormous fountain made from acorn caps. Fresh, sparkling water splashed merrily in a little stream around the fountain whilst yet more water cascaded from a great height.

All around the edge of the drey grew young, fresh pine trees. Hardly believing his luck Rowan launched out into space, grabbing carelessly at an overhanging branch, and happily hanging upside down and swinging from side to side, clasping an acorn here, a horse-chestnut leaf there. In his excitement he was climbing higher and higher into the great drey. Suddenly he came face to face with a pair of big, black eyes.

Rowan stopped in alarm, dropping his treasures. The eyes were dark and menacing. He was afraid. Suddenly there were silver flashes before him, and looking in horror about him he saw hundreds and hundreds of speckled grey squirrels, leaping effortlessly through the air. Rowan was frantic. What was happening, and who were these strange-coloured squirrels who looked so angry?

He turned to run away, but recoiled in horror at the sight behind him. A huge, threatening figure, surely ten times bigger than the others, was descending on him, teeth bared, eyes glistening, claws glowing like pine needles in a sunset.

And then a growl, a deep, powerful growl, so awful that Rowan felt his chest pounding, found he could not draw breath. Panic-stricken, he leapt from the branch to escape, but in his haste he misjudged the distance and tumbled toward the ground - falling, falling..........

What could he do? Somebody *help*!

'Mother!'

'Rowan. Rowan. Do wake up. Whatever were you dreaming about?'

Rowan looked around him in relief. Here he was, safe and sound at home in the drey with his mother close by - as she always was.

'Oh, Mother,' he moaned, 'I had such an awful dream.'

His mother moved closer to him and nudged him with her nose, tickling his chin with her whiskers.

'If you didn't sleep so late, perhaps you would not have bad dreams,' she whispered to him.

Rowan pushed her away playfully, his courage gradually returning. He stretched, and yawned loudly, and then stretched again, and looked up adoringly at his mother. How magnificent she was. Her coat glowed a rich, dark red, and her eyes sparkled like moonlight on a pool of water. Her ears had beautiful tufts and her tail was the bushiest of all the squirrels who lived on the hill. How proud he was of her.

'I'm so hungry,' he sighed, looking hopefully around the drey in case any spare acorns were lying around.

'Well, Rowan,' said his mother reprovingly, 'if you got up on time and went foraging like your brothers and sisters, then your stomach would be full by now.'

Rowan wrinkled his whiskers at his mother, knowing that she

was not really telling him off. He could not help it if he could not wake up when everyone else did. He just needed more sleep than the others.

Leaving the drey he stepped carefully on to the branch outside, stretching first his front legs, and then his back. The bright sunlight made him blink so he sat down and rubbed his eyes. He scratched behind his ear, re-arranged the bush of his tail, and tried to decide where to start the morning groom.

'Go *on*, Rowan,' called his mother, her whiskers twitching, 'by the time you've decided where to start it will be time to go to bed again. Off you go and forage.'

'Yes, mother,' cried Rowan, delighted that his ploy had worked.

'But twice as much grooming tonight,' called his mother as he scampered off. Rowan pretended he had not heard the last remark. By the time bed-time came she would have forgotten all about it. Rowan congratulated himself on being so clever.

High above, Jasmine watched Rowan hurry away, and shook her head despairingly. 'What a tearaway,' she thought. But her eyes softened as she followed her youngest son's progress below. She loved all her infants dearly, of course, but young Rowan, what a rascal. She thought of Petal and Ivy, his sisters, and how self-assured and confident they were. She turned and saw Chestnut and Juniper rolling and tumbling with their friends, so full of life.

She turned again and watched Rowan. How she worried about him, worried that he would not be able to look after himself when she was no longer there. She leaned precariously over the side of the drey when she saw him stumble. She longed to rush straight down to him when a wrinkled root caught him unawares and sent him flying, then smiled to herself as she watched him hurriedly pick himself up, brush the mud off his back, and glance round quickly to see if any other squirrel had seen his fall.

Jasmine leaned back as Rowan looked up to the drey. He had not seen her, but he knew that she was watching him, and he was glad of it.

Ambling along, leisurely as always, Rowan came across

Chestnut and Juniper, busily nuzzling amongst roots and nuts. 'Look out,' cried Juniper, 'hide your acorns!'

'Oh, Juniper,' cried Rowan, 'don't be unfair.'

'Unfair, he says,' Juniper called to Chestnut, and began rapidly gathering together his food collection.

Rowan looked crestfallen. He was so hungry, and Juniper had all those lovely acorns.

Chestnut chuckled. 'Go on, Juniper, give the poor little chap a few.' Putting his nose to the ground he nudged a few nuts towards Rowan. Grudgingly Juniper did likewise.

'Really, Rowan, you must learn to fend for yourself.' Although Juniper tried to sound stern he could not help licking Rowan's ear and playfully pulling his whiskers. There was no animosity in this family; both Chestnut and Juniper thought the world of their rather lazy and exasperating younger brother.

'Thanks Juniper. Thanks Ches,' said Rowan as he eagerly began to munch the offerings.

There was silence as the three crunched, sucked and chewed their way through the feast before them. It had been a mild winter and food was plentiful. None of them had ever experienced real hunger.

It was a lovely morning. The sun was shining and Rowan felt the warmth upon his back. A blackbird called to his mate in the tree above and a brightly-coloured robin flew close by with a juicy worm in its mouth. Rowan paused to suck at the blades of grass under the tree, still wet from the early morning dew.

'Ches,' mumbled Rowan, trying to eat and talk at the same time, 'is there such a thing as a giant acorn?'

'It is quite possible,' Chestnut replied, feeling important. Rowan always looked upon him as a knowledgeable adult, but quite often he found himself out of his depth with Rowan's continual questions.

'I recall once seeing an acorn as big as this,' said Juniper, holding his paws apart and widening them more and more as Rowan gasped.

'I've heard it said,' informed Chestnut, 'that if it wasn't for us squirrels eating the acorns, they would just keep on growing and growing. It is certainly a useful job we do, eating them.'

'Yes, I see,' said Rowan thoughtfully, 'but do you think an acorn could grow as big, say,' and he looked quickly around him, 'as a mountain?'

There were peals of laughter from behind. All three turned to see a group of older squirrels who had obviously been taking great delight in listening to the conversation.

'Do you mind?' said Chestnut indignantly, 'this is a private conversation.'

One of the squirrels stepped forward. Rowan could see from the small tufts on his ears that he was a young adult.

'Do you think,' mimicked the squirrel, 'that an acorn could grow as big as a mountain?'

Again the older squirrels laughed. Rowan felt uncomfortable. Chestnut and Juniper were strangely silent.

Rowan stepped forward. 'Well,' he asked quietly, 'is there?'

The squirrel began preening his whiskers. 'There may be,' he whispered, 'in Invader Country.'

All the other squirrels gasped, and there were low mumblings and tails began to bush out and twitch.

Rowan looked at his brothers in confusion. They too looked horrified. Juniper's teeth were chattering.

'Where on earth is Invader Country?' asked Rowan innocently.

Suddenly there was a lot of noise. The other squirrels were snorting and making strange sounds. One opened his mouth and made a noise like an angry magpie. They ran backwards and forwards and then after urgent whispers abruptly turned and began to move away, mumbling and chucking to each other.

'Don't go,' cried Rowan, 'please tell me.'

The squirrel who had spoken earlier turned quickly. 'Just beware the Grey Invaders.' Then his tail was up, and he was gone.

Rowan turned to his brothers and was bewildered by the fear he saw in their eyes. 'Juniper, who are these Grey Inv.........'

'Quiet!' yelled Chestnut, cuffing Rowan across the ears. 'You are never, *never* to mention that name.'

'Why not?' asked Rowan.

'Don't ask. Just don't ask. Do you understand?'

'Yes,' said Rowan miserably, rubbing his ears.

'Let's not stay here,' said Chestnut, 'it's getting dark. I think a storm is coming.'

Juniper shivered. Rowan looked up but the sky seemed bright and cheerful to him. He followed his brothers as they turned in the direction of the drey and began scampering towards the home tree. Rowan grabbed a plump, shiny acorn and went to give it to Jasmine. Perhaps she would tell him about the Grey Invaders. He rubbed his ears again, still surprised and confused by his brothers' reactions to such an ordinary name. In fact, he liked the sound of it. The Grey Invaders. They sounded so interesting. So exciting. So...so dangerous.

'The Grey Invaders,' he whispered, listening to the sound of the name. Were these the squirrels that he saw in his nightmare?

CHAPTER TWO

Rowan was thinking. It was not often that any one subject stayed long in his mind, but he was completely engrossed in this one. Who or what were the Grey Invaders and why wouldn't anyone talk to him about them? It made him all the more curious.

Chestnut had given him another clip round the ears when he had asked about them again. Juniper just ground his teeth in the most annoying manner. Petal and Ivy turned their backs on him when he asked them. Even his mother! What a strange reaction from her. She had actually told Chestnut off, although it had been nothing to do with him really.

Rowan recalled the conversation he had overheard between his mother and Chestnut.

'Who was it who spoke about them, Chestnut?'

'I don't know. One of the older squirrels.'

'I will not hear the name mentioned. Do you understand me, Chestnut?'

'Yes, mother.'

'And you are certainly not to talk to Rowan about them. He is too young.'

'But he's got to know sooner or later.'

A loud sigh. 'I know, you are probably right. But not just yet. Please Chestnut. Not for a while.'

'But he asks so many questions, Mother.'

Jasmine moved closer to Chestnut and whispered urgently to him. 'Forgive me, son. I'm sorry I was so angry with you. But don't you see? You and Juniper, and Ivy and Petal, you could all understand. But Rowan is too young at the moment. How can I tell him that they killed his father?'

It was at that point that Rowan had run away. He had run and run until he was exhausted, and now here he was sitting at the foot of this great oak tree, wondering why the Grey Invaders killed his father. He remembered the sleek, proud parent who had been so devoted to his mother. He thought of how he used to follow him through the woods, and listen to his father explaining all about the wood. He remembered the whole family resting in the cool of an evening after a long, hot summer. It was in this very tree, he recalled, that he had first recognised the colour of his coat from the colour of the leaves that autumn evening. He had looked up and seen clouds of orange, brown and red and wondered where the green leaves had gone to. His father had smiled and explained to him what happened to the trees in the changing seasons. He had told Rowan that his coat would be the colour of autumn leaves, like his mother's and his brothers' and sisters'. Rowan had rolled in the leaves and laughed and chattered and everyone had grinned at him. That was such a happy time.

He remembered, too, his father explaining to Ivy and Petal about all the other animals that lived in the wood, the dormouse, the vole, the rabbits, and about the birds that nested in the trees, just like squirrels. He thought of the rats. He had seen them once and his father had told him never to speak to them. Were they the Grey Invaders?

And why was his father dead?

Rowan began miserably chewing on an acorn. He had not eaten since he had left the drey that morning. His mind was as foggy as a winter morning and he felt so tired he could hardly keep his eyes open. He curled up slowly, wrapping his tail around him, and fell into a deep sleep.

Not far away, watching his brother, squatted Juniper. He was savouring the taste of a mushroom and enjoying the sensation of it in his mouth. He wondered what to do, whether to go back to the drey and tell his mother, or stay and watch over Rowan.

Juniper hated making decisions. Usually Chestnut led, and he followed. He sat for some time listening, watching, waiting. All was quiet. Rowan was breathing gently. Fast asleep. Quietly Juniper crept away, back to the drey to report that his runaway brother was safe and sound, sleeping under the great oak tree.

After Juniper had left, Jasmine sat thinking for a while. She knew she worried too much about Rowan. He was the youngest. The baby. Why did it always seem to be him that got into trouble? He still needed to be watched over. He was not ready yet to face sadness and death.

Thoughtfully she patted the bedding of the drey. Perhaps she should go to him, be there when he woke up, in case he started asking questions again.

He asks so many questions, Chestnut had said. Was she wrong to keep it from him? Chestnut probably thought so. She sighed. Maybe Rowan was growing up right before her eyes and she had not noticed it. Or perhaps chose not to notice.

Nodding to herself, she left the drey and made her way to the great oak. She had to wait for some time before Rowan eventually woke up.

'Mother,' he yawned, 'how did you know where I was?'

'Never mind that now,' she said softly, 'I want to talk to you, Rowan.'

Rowan immediately sat up and stretched, scratched, and yawned again. 'I know I shouldn't have run away, Mother. I won't do it again. I promise.'

Jasmine smiled and nuzzled up to her son. 'Oh, Rowan,' she whispered, 'it's not about that.'

Rowan looked alert. 'Is it about Father?'

Jasmine's tail jerked and her ears twitched nervously. 'Yes, it's time I told you what happened.'

Rowan said, without thinking, 'But you told Chestnut I must never know.'

Jasmine was surprised. 'You mean you were listening?'

Rowan was silent.

'Is that why you ran away?'

Rowan looked sullen. 'I think so.'

Jasmine gave a deep sigh. 'Come here Rowan, and sit by me. I want to tell you a story.'

Rowan moved to his mother's side and lay down beside her. Jasmine preened her tail, stroked her whiskers, and taking a deep breath, she began:

'You know that we live here on Tolls Hill? Well, this is actually an island. In fact, away over there is another island. Long ago, when you were very young we red squirrels lived on one island and grey squirrels lived on the other.'

Rowan sat up. 'Grey squirrels?' he said in surprise. Jasmine nodded. 'What exactly is a grey squirrel, Mother?' he asked tentatively.

Jasmine thought for a moment. 'Do you remember during last winter we all woke up one morning and everything was covered in fog?'

'Yes,' nodded Rowan, 'everything was the same colour.'

'That's right,' replied Jasmine, 'there were no colours. Everything was grey.'

Rowan looked thoughtful. 'Everything was grey,' he repeated.

Jasmine continued.

'The Queen of the Red Squirrel Island was Amber, a magnificent red female, whose coat was so shiny that when the sun shone, it dazzled all who looked upon it. Her tail was the brightest and bushiest that had ever been seen, and was the envy of all the other squirrels.'

Rowan looked at his mother adoringly. 'But not as bushy as yours,' he said softly.

Jasmine shushed him, and Rowan lay down again quietly.

'Amber, as I said, was the Queen. It was she who said where the tree houses were to be built, and where the nut stores would be.'

Rowan started to speak, but was quietened by a look from his mother.

'On the other island, where the grey squirrels lived, was their King. He was called Greybeard. He was easily twice as big as any other squirrel, almost a giant. Yet he was gentle and kind. His coat was silver, and was so thick that birds would follow him waiting for the opportunity to steal some of it for their nests. He was a great fighter and bore many scars. Some say he had one scar for each victory. Well, he must have had at least twenty scars all over his body.'

'Phew!' exclaimed Rowan in wonder. He could feel the hairs on the back of his tail standing on end. He snuggled closer to his mother.

'The grey squirrels and the red squirrels never spoke. They lived their own lives, each ignoring the existence of the other. One day, Amber and Greybeard met whilst foraging. They fell in love, and used to meet secretly by a little brook that ran between the two islands. They were so happy, Rowan, those two lovers. The red squirrels had never known their Queen so cheerful, and the grey squirrels were so surprised that their great leader had no more interest in fighting. But one day a mean, miserable squirrel with a dull, grey coat and a horrible scar across the side of his face decided to follow Greybeard to see why he was so changed. This squirrel, whose name was Scarface, really wanted to be the ruler and was determined to discredit Greybeard in front of the other grey squirrels.

So it was that Scarface came across Amber and Greybeard. Scarface was appalled that a grey squirrel was with a red squirrel, and he attacked Greybeard. There was a terrible fight. Although Greybeard finally won and chased his opponent away, Scarface returned quickly to the grey squirrel island and immediately called a meeting of all the squirrels. He told them what he had seen, telling the grey squirrels that their leader had been with the enemies on red squirrel island, and that he was a traitor. By the time Greybeard finally returned, all the squirrels had turned against him, and he was chased off the island.

Jasmine paused and glanced at Rowan. His mouth was partially open, and not a whisker moved. She continued:

'Not knowing where to go or what to do, Greybeard went to find Amber. Together they told the red squirrels the story, and also told them that they were in love. The red squirrels took to Greybeard straight away, amazed that he had mellowed Amber so much. They insisted that they should live together on red squirrel island, which they did. A magnificent drey was built in the tallest tree, and there Amber lived with Greybeard. Previously, you see, there had always been lots of disagreements because some squirrels did not like the greys but others wanted to be friends. So when Greybeard came to live with us everyone seemed happy, and the island became a happy and a gentle place to live.

Some time later, on Grey Squirrel island, Scarface was becoming bored. Now he was ruler, and no other squirrel was brave enough to fight him. So one day, when a large squirrel called Thistle came to see him and told him that Amber and Greybeard were living together on red squirrel island, Scarface was elated. He gathered together all the adult fighters and told them that they were going to invade Red Squirrel Island and kill Greybeard.'

Rowan squealed. 'The Grey Invaders!'

Jasmine nodded. 'Soon the grey squirrels became so incensed with the plans for the invasion and the 'big fight', that Scarface could hardly control them. Early one morning, they attacked. The red squirrels were not expecting them, and hundreds were killed, torn apart by the grey squirrels' cruel teeth. Everywhere was chaos. All the adult red squirrels were trying vainly to protect their families, but the Grey Invaders were merciless. They killed any red squirrels, fathers, mothers, and even infants. It was a terrible time.'

Jasmine stopped suddenly and Rowan heard her catch her breath and heard a little squeak in her throat. He nuzzled her silently.

'It was Spring,' she stammered, emotion choking her voice, 'but it seemed like the end of autumn.....everywhere was red......' - she looked up - 'It was as though the leaves were bleeding, and the grass and the ground itself was dying.......'

After a moment she composed herself, and continued:

'Dreys were torn to pieces, and when they found the drey of Amber and Greybeard it was shredded and thrown into the wind, and grey squirrels stamped on it and yelled "*Victory, victory.*" '

Jasmine paused again, and breathed deeply. Rowan was horrified, and the sadness showed plainly in his eyes. He gulped and felt the tightness in his throat.

'What happened to Amber and Greybeard?'

'They were never found. The Grey Invaders must have killed them.'

Rowan hesitated. 'And Father?' he ventured.

Jasmine sighed. 'Your father took us to a safe place and went back to help the others. When he did not return, I went to look for him. I found his body not far from where he had left us. It was lying beside the body of a grey squirrel. They had fought to the death.'

Rowan tried to speak, but the words would not come. Instead he found himself huddled up against his mother, murmuring 'Tuk, Tuk, Tuk,' as he had when he was very young.

CHAPTER THREE

The hill was busy today. Young infants were rolling and tumbling in the long grass, while groups of adults rooted and explored amongst the tree roots. Several older females busily scurried back and forth to their dreys, some carrying twigs and branches, others carrying ferns and dried grass.

There was a loud shriek as a young adult hurried by, closely followed by another squirrel in hot pursuit. A few of the adults momentarily ceased their chewing to watch the couple racing. Noses quivered and tails jerked and then eating began in earnest again.

It was a beautiful day on the hill. The sun shone brightly, gently warming the squirrels as they moved in its brightness. Food was plentiful. The females chattered eagerly to one another, while the older males, ignoring their fellow squirrels, kept lone vigils around the edge of the hill, constantly watching for danger.

Jasmine surveyed the scene from her drey where she was resting. She had spent much of the previous night comforting Rowan, and had had little sleep. Her body ached today and as she looked around her she wondered if she would ever tire of enjoying the wonderful scenery around her. It was mid-summer and the days were long and balmy. She stretched her tired limbs and moved slightly so that she could see over the hill, past the watching patrollers, right over to Grey Squirrel Island. She watched the swallows diving and cavorting and saw a hawk head for the island. Some grey squirrel would die today, she thought tiredly.

Then she looked back at the scene below her. She could not blame them for not wanting to move away after the invasion. It was a wonderful place to live, familiar, a place that offered plentiful food supplies, good shelter, and a place with memories. After the grey squirrels had gone, leaving the carnage behind, the survivors that returned were frightened and confused. There were no male adults left to tell them what to do, except for those that had been wounded. They were so shocked they could hardly speak.

Amber and Greybeard had disappeared. 'What could we have done?' sighed Jasmine sadly.

And what would they do if it happened again? This time the patrollers would be vigilant. They would never be taken by surprise again. They were all as safe as they could be anywhere. At least, she hoped so. Finally her eyes closed, and she slept.

Rowan stretched out under a pine tree. It was so warm and comfortable. The ground smelled fresh and inviting. Not far away a few rabbits played on the green turf. Tolls Hill was a place where squirrel and rabbit lived side by side in harmony.

Rowan rolled from side to side, looking first at the sky, then at the trees and then at the bottom of the pine tree. He was full of good food, and now he was tired. He felt the warmth of the sun on his back, and he yawned loudly. He closed one eye and with the other lazily watched the rabbits playing tag. He smiled as they bounded around, jumping over each other and squealing in delight. He really was quite warm. He would have to move into the shade of the wood soon.

When Rowan awoke he thought his body was on fire. His mouth felt as though there were a great chunk of bark in it so that he could hardly breathe. There was such a hammering in his head he wondered if a stoat were carrying him over a pile of rocks and banging his head against them. He tried to focus on the familiar sights around him, but everything was a blur. He wondered if the pine tree had fallen on him because his legs would not move and his tail was stuck fast.

Gradually he remembered lying down beneath the tree. The sun had been overhead but now it was somewhere behind the hill. When he tried to swallow he realised the chunk of bark in his mouth was his swollen tongue. He realised then that he must have fallen asleep in the sun and that he had to get a drink of water. Water... soft, and gentle.... refreshing, sparkling, life-saving.

Slowly, painfully, he dragged himself into the wood, inch by inch. Gradually the cool of the forest refreshed him and he began to feel his body again. How he ached. How his head hurt.

He stumbled into the wood, not knowing whether he was heading towards the drey or away from the hill. The scent of the wood was strange, unfamiliar. He did not know whether he was imagining the strange smells or whether his nose was behaving strangely too, like his tongue. He staggered and fell.

Chestnut and Juniper were sitting side by side beneath a towering pine and were casually stripping long slivers of bark from the tree and munching thoughtfully as they discussed the situation.

'He knows then,' declared Juniper.

Chestnut nodded silently, his cheeks bulging. 'He had to know sometime. Might as well be now.'

Chestnut swallowed with difficulty and licked his lips. 'Mmm. That was good. Yes, you're right. At least we don't have to hide it from him any more.'

'How do you think he took it?' asked Juniper.

Chestnut considered for a moment and then began to nibble at the grass at his feet, collecting tiny fragments of broken bark. 'I think he'll be alright. Mother sat with him all night and I saw him rolling around earlier. Knowing Rowan, he's already forgotten about them.'

'I remember when I first knew,' mused Juniper. 'It was a sad day for me. I went to the top of the hill over there, where you can see Grey Squirrel Island, and shouted and screamed until I had no breath left. It made no difference, they could not hear me.'

'But you felt much better?'

'I did,' nodded Juniper.

'I decided to go over there, once,' revealed Chestnut, amused at the amazed look on his brother's face. 'I did. I even went as far as the bottom of the hill. But then I could not bring myself to go any further. And then I thought, father died protecting the hill for us, why should I want to leave? So I came back.'

'What did Mother say?'

'She never knew.'

'Oh.' Juniper was disappointed. He thought Chestnut was going to tell him a really exciting story, but nothing had happened.

'Has anyone ever left Tolls Hill?' he asked.

'I don't think so,' replied Chestnut. 'Why would anyone want to? We've got everything we want here, food, shelter, we can see clearly all around for danger. No one knows what's out there....beyond....' he looked out over the hill, wondering.

'But what if they come back?' queried Juniper, tearing another piece of bark from the tree and greedily stuffing it into his mouth.

'Why should they? As far as they know, we're all dead.'

A shiver went down Juniper's back making his fur stand on end and his tail twitch uncontrollably.

It was some time later that Rowan awoke again. He felt much better, although still terribly thirsty. Never again, he thought, would he fall asleep lying in the sunshine.

Although his body still hurt he knew he must find water. He shook his head as he heard strange noises in his ears. He turned his head this way and that, convinced that something was screeching at him. But there was nothing nearby. Feeling dis-orientated he began to wander further and further into the cool wood. Pine trees loomed up beside him, before him, and behind him. The ground smelled unfamiliar, like rotting fruit. Strange shadows gathered round him. Suddenly feeling afraid, he leapt up into a nearby tree, scurrying quickly to the top branches to see just where he was.

Rowan gasped out loud. All he could see around him were the tops of the pines. Where was the hill? Which way had he come? He found himself grinding his teeth as Juniper had done, and his tail swished backwards and forwards uncontrollably.

He tried to keep calm. Tried to climb high enough to see over the trees but there was nothing familiar anywhere. His ears strained for sounds that he could recognise, but the wood was silent and still.

Then his nose began to wrinkle as he smelled the air. It was not just the dampness of the wood he could smell. There was water nearby, he was sure of it. Excitement mounting within him, he rushed down the tree and stretched high on his hind legs in the moist moss of the ground. Now he was sure he could hear water bubbling and gurgling. Following the sound he hurried through the thickening trees. He ran and ran until his legs felt weak and his feet were sore. But there was no doubt. Water was nearby.

All at once there was a clearing in the wood. Sure enough a stream trickled through the centre of the sunlit opening. Rowan let out a gasp of delight and skipped joyfully, albeit painfully, to the water's edge.

He sucked in the cool, refreshing nectar until his stomach was bursting. Almost immediately he began to feel his tongue again as the crystal clear water soothed his burning throat. Letting out a long sigh of pleasure and relief he carefully edged his feet into the stream. It felt wonderful.

Laughing delightedly he then put his tail in too and watched in amazement as it soaked up the liquid and began to sink. When he flicked it, hundreds of drops of water, like an April shower, splashed over him. The water was so cool and inviting that, with only a moment's hesitation, Rowan jumped into the middle of the stream and began to swim around. First he went from one bank to the other, at first unsure of the unfamiliar water and pulling himself quickly on to the firm ground. Then he would jump in again, gradually becoming more confident.

Soon he was diving, surfacing a few feet away, blowing out a thin stream of water, and then diving down again. He opened his eyes under water and saw long, waving plants beckoning to him. He rolled around them and then kicked with his back legs and sprang to the surface time after time until he was exhausted.

Although his body was tired he was having such fun he could not resist one last dive. Down, down he went, in and out of the waving plants. He loved the way they rubbed his body as he passed through them, as though they were playing the game too. But suddenly it was no longer a game. One of the weeds had caught his foot and would not let go. He pulled and struggled, and as he gasped bubbles of water raced from his mouth to the surface.

He began to panic because he could not breathe. 'Let me go, let me go,' he tried to yell, but every time he opened his mouth to shout the water rushed in and made him choke.

Struggling and gasping, he tore at the plants with his paws until finally he was free. He pulled himself out of the water and splashed and kicked with his feet while he puffed and coughed, and laughed and gasped, all at the same time.

When he stopped shaking he realised that he was cold. He shook himself thoroughly, watching in amazement as the droplets flew through the air around him, like hundreds of sparkling dewdrops.

Just then he noticed a very tall tree, and quickly skimmed up it to the very top, balancing precariously on a broken branch. He squinted his eyes and stretched his neck as far as he could and, yes, there in the distance, he saw the hill.

He looked carefully all around him, trying to work out the route home. He saw the tall and spindly pines, and the young saplings, and he kept looking first at the hill, then to the stream, and back again, until he was sure he had memorised the way. Rowan thought of his father then, for it was he who had taught him how to find his way in the wood. Always look at the sun, he had said, and read the tops of the trees. Always keep going to the uppermost branches and keep the sun in the same place and you will find your way home. Rowan searched for the sun now. It was getting late and it was very low in the sky, but he could just make out the orange glow ahead.

'Oh, Father, I miss you,' he sighed. But he was proud now and pleased that he had listened to the advice that his father had given to him.

For after all, here he was alone in the middle of a big, dark, wood, and he was able to find his way home again. He would tell Mother as soon as he got back to the drey. She would be so pleased with him.

Leaping down the tree Rowan landed lightly on the ground

below. 'Why,' thought Rowan to himself, 'I climbed that tree as well as Chestnut or Juniper.'

He was very pleased with himself. Pausing before heading back through the wood, he turned and looked again at the special place that he had found. Better still, this would be his secret place. He would tell no one about it. He would come here whenever he wanted to be alone, and he would swim, and sunbathe, and forage, just as long as he wanted.

Triumphantly he turned and headed back into the wood. He was confident of the way now, and as he skipped and jumped he noticed more and more about the trees. He noted the old oak with a broken trunk and the large spruce beside it like a giant squirrel's tail, the row of young pines standing like sentinels, tall, erect and proud. He memorised the birch with the gleaming white bark and the huge, huge pine with a mountain of cones beneath it. He raced up a tree and looked back to the clearing by the stream, and then ahead again to the sinking sun. He grabbed a pine cone and bit a large chunk out of the side and dropped it to the ground, listening with satisfaction as it bumped and twirled its way to the moss below. Then he leapt through the air, sailing from tree-top to tree-top, chuckling loudly to himself. No, he would never get lost in this wood again.

Many days of foraging had passed. Every day Rowan headed for his secret place. Every day Jasmine wondered where her youngest son disappeared to. She was pleased, in a way, that he was becoming more independent, but she was just a little concerned that no one seemed to know where he went.

It became obvious that Rowan did not wish to confide in either his mother or his brothers and sisters, shying away from probing questions, until eventually Jasmine accepted that her Rowan was growing up and she asked him no more. Juniper and Chestnut were impressed by his ability to amuse himself, but were both more than a little curious. If they were honest, they would admit to missing their brother and his cute but frustrating little ways.

Life was good for Rowan now. He knew that everyone longed to know where he was going each day as he sped away towards the wood, flicking his tail in defiance and looking behind him as he went. When he reached the very edge of the hill, at the entrance to the wood, he stopped and began to feed busily, until all the other squirrels forgot him. Then in an instant he dashed away into the undergrowth. By the time the others had realised he had gone, it was too late.

Rowan chattered to himself as he ambled through the wood.

'Hello, Mr Pine Tree,' he said to one tree, and 'Hello, Mr Very Tall and Thin Tree,' to another. And so he would carry on until he reached the clearing, his secret place.

Squeaking with delight he ran across the grass and jumped straight into the water, swimming madly round and round in circles. He dived, and then sprang up through the water, gasping in air, and then dived again. He swam to the opposite bank, pulled himself out, and then turned and jumped right back in again, splashing around in the water and watching as the ripples that his tail made churned up the surface and made the reflections wobble and dance.

He decided to see how far he could swim under water, taking every care to avoid the weeds, of course. With a deep breath he sank beneath the surface and began to paddle his legs up and down, propelling himself forwards. He winked at a startled frog and chuckled as a newt watched him in amazement. The long leaves of the water plants tried to grab him but he flicked his tail at them and swam on. He explored logs and giant stones that had obviously been under water for a long time, enjoying the feel of the soft wood and the cold stone.

He was a long way from the familiar bank, and realised that he must have swum quite a way down the stream. Mustering all his energy he swam slowly to the bank and dragged himself on to the solid ground. He lay wheezing and struggling to breathe normally, his body heavy and clumsy with all the water in his fur. He had not got the energy to shake himself dry yet, he needed to rest for a while.

As he lay panting, he thought he heard a strange noise. Perhaps it was the water in his ears, he thought, shaking his head. It was still there. It sounded like the 'chuck, chuck' of another squirrel.

Slowly he turned his head in the direction of the noise. There, squatting in the green grass, watching him with wide eyes, was a young squirrel.

'My goodness,' said the stranger, 'what a start you gave me.'

Rowan was speechless.

'Are you dead?' asked the stranger.

Rowan shook his head, for still he could not speak. He opened his mouth but nothing came out - his tongue would not move. Despite his wet coat, he felt the hairs on his body standing on end. He laid back his ears in fear and his teeth were chattering and grinding.

Suddenly he remembered his terrible dream, and thought of his father. The squirrel that sat before him was grey from head to foot. The colour of a foggy winter's morning... he thought.... a Grey Invader.

A Grey Invader

CHAPTER FOUR

'You're not very friendly, are you?' said the squirrel.

Rowan stuttered and stammered but his mouth would not work properly and he found himself unable to respond.

'My name is Fern. What's yours?'

Still no reply.

'If you don't want to talk, then I'll go away.' And with a defiant flick of her tail she turned away.

'Are you.....' spluttered Rowan, '......are you a Grey Invader?'

'A what?' asked the stranger, pausing.

Rowan sat up, shook himself vigorously, and moved closer. Swallowing slowly he forced himself to speak.

'Are you a Grey Invader?'

The squirrel shook her head in confusion. 'What utter rubbish you talk. I told you, my name is Fern, and I live over there.' She looked behind her.

Rowan gasped. The other side of the wood! Should he run away or attack or play innocent and find out more?

'Where you live,' said Rowan carefully, 'is it called Grey Squirrel Island?'

'How did you know that?' came the reply.

Rowan sat down again and looked carefully around him. There was no movement. He and this female were totally alone. He had nothing to fear.

'I know all about grey squirrels,' said Rowan vehemently, 'I know they are vicious and that they kill red squirrels. And I know about Scarface and Thistle. And I know about Greybeard and Amber. So there!'

The grey squirrel sat down and began to scratch, stretching her long slender leg to her ear and rubbing casually.

'I don't know what you are talking about. I certainly don't kill other squirrels, and I'm not surprised you know Scarface and Thistle. Doesn't everyone? As for Greybeard and Amber, I've never heard of them and I think you're making them up.'

Rowan looked indignant and opened his mouth to interrupt but she gave him a piercing glare and he stopped abruptly.

'And anyway,' she continued, 'who are you, and why are you such a funny colour?'

'I'm not the one who is a funny colour,' retorted Rowan, 'you are.'

'How rude.'

The stranger swivelled round and began to move away, hesitated momentarily and then looked back over her shoulder at Rowan, calling to him as she went:

'If you can speak nicely to me, I'll be back tomorrow.'

Rowan watched her go, but once again found himself unable to say anything. His mouth was working and his tongue moved but no sounds came out.

She called again, 'But if you're not going to be nice, then I shan't come.'

Rowan thought quickly. He could have the whole of Red Squirrel Island waiting here tomorrow and they could attack this stranger and kill her. He winced. He hated violence. One major disadvantage would be that everyone would find his secret place. Perhaps he should find out more first. He might even be able to capture Scarface and Thistle. A shiver shot down his back.

'My name's Rowan,' he yelled. But she had gone. He had no way of knowing if she had heard him. He would have to see if she turned up tomorrow.

Rowan had a restless night, and was the first of the family to wake when the sun rose the next morning. Quickly he left the drey and perched on a nearby branch, sitting himself comfortably and beginning the morning groom. He took a deep breath and felt the dew in his nostrils. The sky was the colour of spring bluebells and the sun smiled at him like a giant daffodil. Bees buzzed around his ears and he playfully brushed them away.

Below him the rabbits were out, stretching and yawning and beginning their early morning graze in the long grass. A sparrow with a white wing perched on a hanging pine cone and watched with him. He saw the magpies squabbling and pecking each other

Beginning their early morning graze

as they flew past, and
sat silently as a mother vole hurried her children past the skittish rabbits. Somewhere a skylark sang and a gentle breeze rustled the leaves of the trees around them. Rowan winked at the sparrow, and it cocked its head and winked back before flying away.

Today was special, and Rowan was determined to look his best when he met the grey squirrel again. He yawned loudly, and scratched, and then began meticulously grooming his tail, licking and chewing the matted fur until it gradually lay in place. He preened his whiskers until they shone in the morning sunlight, and polished his claws until they were the colour of corn in the harvest.

For most of the night he had thought of his secret place, and now his secret friend. He wondered about where she lived, and what her family were like, and longed to know whether all grey squirrels were vicious, like those who had killed his father. He paused from his grooming and considered this point. He felt a terrible hatred for those animals that had so mercilessly slaughtered innocent squirrels. His tail bristled and his teeth began to gnash as he thought of all his mother had told him. There was no doubt about it, he hated all grey squirrels. He would find this Scarface and Thistle and he would kill them himself. He would avenge his father's death.

But then he thought again of the young grey squirrel that he had met. Fern, that was her name. A nice name too, and he really rather liked her silvery coat.

He began to clean again, now concentrating on his red fur, pleased with the shine that had been left on his tail.

'Well, my goodness,' exclaimed Jasmine, coming to the edge of the drey and seeing her youngest son so busy. Rowan was startled and nearly fell off the branch. He looked shyly at his mother, and then continued with his licking and patting and pawing.

'I really don't believe what I am seeing,' said Jasmine again, shaking her head in disbelief.

Rowan looked up, feeling slightly annoyed. 'Really, Mother,' he replied, 'what is the matter?'

There was a rustle behind Jasmine, and Juniper appeared behind her, looking tired and dishevelled. He looked in surprise at Rowan.

'Am I dreaming?' he asked mischievously, 'or have we all overslept?'

'What is it?' asked Chestnut from inside the drey.

'I think it's Rowan, but I don't believe it,' called Juniper.

Then Ivy and Petal were there too, all looking astounded. Rowan was disconcerted by all the attention his early morning start was causing.

'He's obviously sick,' declared Juniper matter-of-factly.

'I am not sick,' retorted Rowan.

'Then what on earth are you doing up and about this early in the morning?' asked Chestnut, edging out of the drey behind everyone else.

Rowan returned to his grooming, wondering how best to reply. He was anxious not to arouse any suspicions.

'It is such a lovely day,' he said quietly, 'that I thought I would go foraging early and bring some acorns back for Mother.' Jasmine looked pleased.

'Oh, Rowan,' she said, 'what a lovely thought.'

'Huh,' muttered Juniper, 'acorns my foot.'

'I did, Juniper,' cried Rowan, unhappy that he had lied, but anxious that no one should ask any more questions.

'There's more to this, you know,' said Juniper, determined to find out what was going on. Jasmine turned to her elder sons and with her back to Rowan so that he could not see her face, winked secretly at them and said loudly,

'Rowan is right. It is a lovely day and we are all wasting it. Let's start grooming, and then we can all go foraging together.'

Juniper and Chestnut mumbled and grumbled and spread out beside Rowan, whilst Ivy and Petal whispered and giggled together. Jasmine hissed at them and abruptly they moved out on to the surrounding branches, licking and preening, but still casting glances at each other.

Rowan looked crestfallen. At any other time he would have loved a family outing. But not today. Not when he had arranged to meet Fern.

The rest of the family, sniggering and chattering amongst themselves, had not noticed Rowan's worried expression.

Slowly Rowan began to stretch and move, trying to think of an excuse to leave the family gathering. Then he found himself whispering her name. Fern. Fern. He really did like that name.

It was not long before Juniper and Chestnut had noticed the way Rowan was behaving and began nudging each other. Soon Ivy and Petal joined in and eventually the whole family were laughing and tussling and teasing until they all tumbled to the ground below, laughing and gasping in their excitement. Jasmine gave up trying to get everyone to clean up first, and they all bounded away together. Juniper had grudgingly agreed to show them his secret store and Jasmine, Ivy and Petal were astounded at the number of pine cones he had collected together. Chestnut was pleased that his brother had agreed to share the feast, and nudged Juniper gently.

'I'll help you collect some more later,' he whispered.

Juniper cheered up then. Actually they were rather having fun. Ivy and Petal could be quite amusing sometimes. They were laughing and joking together, and Jasmine was listening quietly to their chatter, occasionally joining in with her daughters. Juniper and Chestnut ambled over to them, and there were squeals of laughter as Ivy related the story of how a young squirrel who lived in the middle of the wood had been found sound asleep, hanging upside down from a branch.

Rowan was not really listening. All morning he had been trying to think of a good reason to leave, but to no avail. He had been feeding with the others, and now he was too tired and too full to think any more. He yawned noisily, and then stretched luxuriously under the shade of a nearby pine tree. Jasmine saw him and soon joined him, lying down by his side. The pair were quickly joined by the others, and it was not long before the whole family were fast asleep.

There was little activity on the hill when the sun was high in the sky. Squirrels liked to get up early and then catch up on lost sleep during the heat of the day. The rabbits, too, were asleep in the burrows, and even the noisy magpies were resting in the tree-tops. Rowan, having had such a restless night, was exhausted, and slept heavily. He woke abruptly when he heard loud snorting and growling. Something was wrong. Suddenly everyone was awake, and Jasmine and Chestnut were sniffing the air and listening to the noises, trying to find out what was happening.

Suddenly there was a shadow overhead, a black shadow was moving towards them. Rowan stood still, transfixed by the strange and unknown sight.

He could see nothing except the large black image moving effortlessly across the turf. Ivy and Petal squealed, and looking into the sky he saw a frightening sight. A large animal with huge arms, suspended high above him. A cruel mouth, hard and pointed, glinted in the sunshine, and big, piercing eyes scoured the ground below. Then the animal stopped gliding, and hovered directly above the family.

'Hawk. Hawk,' shrilled Chestnut. 'Run for your lives. Run for your lives.'

He dashed into the wood, closely followed by Ivy and Petal.

'Juniper, Rowan,' called Jasmine urgently, 'quickly, into the wood with Chestnut.'

'Hawk! Hawk!'

Juniper turned and began to gallop after his brother, closely followed by Jasmine. Suddenly he stopped, causing Jasmine to run straight into him.

'Where is Rowan?'

They turned quickly and to their horror saw Rowan still standing gazing at the hawk. Looking upwards they saw that the hawk was talking to Rowan.

'Don't move, little squirrel,' it whined, 'just stay right where you are. I'm your friend. I won't hurt you.'

In a flash as quick as a lightning bolt Juniper streaked back to Rowan and bit him sharply behind his ear. Rowan jumped.

'Quickly,' shrieked Juniper, 'don't listen to him. Just run.'

Rowan ran, and heard his brother right behind him. They heard a cry from above and as they ran they felt the wind from the great bird's wings as he flew towards them. Juniper could hear the great monster closing behind. He ran faster, faster than ever before. He felt the talons rake his back, but they did not grip.

Panic-stricken, they reached the wood and rushed up to the others, their breath rasping in their throats. Jasmine quickly gathered them all together as the angry animal in the sky shrieked and shouted at them. It rose high into the sky and dived down and down upon the cowering family, screeching and whining at them. Jasmine gently reassured her family, chukking to them in her motherly way. Soon the great animal tired of them and flew away.

When his teeth had stopped chattering Rowan asked his mother what the animal was.

'A hawk, Rowan,' she whispered.

'What is......a hawk?' he asked hoarsely.

Chestnut interrupted. 'It's a giant bird, Rowan. It flies through the air and can move very, very fast. Sometimes you don't know it's there until it dives at you.'

Jasmine had moved close to Rowan and began gently to lick the ugly wounds on his back. She shook her head as she busily tended to his wounds, pausing frequently as Rowan winced. She knew she would have to do the best she could until they were all safely back in the drey.

'D....dives at you?' stuttered Rowan.

'That's right,' said Jasmine, quieting Chestnut gently, 'It dives at you. You see, Rowan, hawks kill squirrels and eat them.'

Ivy and Petal were crying. Jasmine looked at Chestnut who quickly went to his sisters and began to comfort them.

'But why don't they eat acorns?' asked Rowan, horrified.

'They don't eat the same food as we do,' explained Jasmine. 'They eat animals. They dive on them from above, and kill them with their claws. You must always watch out for them.' Jasmine turned to the rest of her family. 'All of you must be careful.'

Jasmine then went to Juniper and licked him around his eyes and nose.

'Well done, Juniper,' she cooed, 'that was very brave of you. Well done.'

'Yes, well done. Well done, Juniper,' muttered the others as they gathered round their heroic brother. Rowan pushed his way past his mother and stood before his brother.

'You saved my life,' he said. Juniper said nothing. Rowan went to him and rubbed his nose against his chin.

'He was talking to me, you know,' said Rowan.

'I know,' replied Juniper, 'he was trying to fool you.'

'I couldn't move,' mumbled Rowan, beginning to shake violently. Jasmine moved closer and butted him softly. 'Come on. Let's go back to the drey now and look after those wounds properly.'

Rowan followed his mother and Ivy and Petal, side by side, shuffled along behind. Chestnut moved next to Juniper.

'That was very brave of you, Juniper.'

'Thank you,' replied Juniper, very pleased at this praise from his elder brother. 'Shall we go back to the drey together?'

Chestnut nodded, and the two brothers turned and followed the rest of their family.

Jasmine was awake before the storm broke. She had smelt it in the air, and now the drey shook as the distant thunder boomed. Quietly she moved to the edge of the drey to watch. Great streaks of brilliant light broke the darkness. The trees began to vibrate and tremble as the storm moved closer.

Knowingly, Jasmine nodded to the other mothers woken by the oncoming torrent and peering from their warm, dry homes. All along the tree-tops wrinkling noses worked as they assessed the storm and the disruption it was likely to bring.

When the first heavy drops of rain fell she knew that the storm would be bad. The sky became alive with bright lights and the incessant rumblings became more and more threatening. Then the leaves around the drey began to bend and arch as the rain became a torrent. The great old trees groaned and creaked as the wind began to blow and the air became alive with the sound of the forest moaning under the onslaught.

She turned and looked reassuringly at her family as first Chestnut, then Juniper, and then Ivy and Petal joined her.

'It's going to be bad,' said Chestnut. No one else spoke. The noises around became so loud that they could not have heard anyway. Loud cracks echoed in the night air as thick branches snapped and fell, crashing to the ground below. The drey quaked and rocked and soon a continual stream of water cascaded past the watching squirrels.

Each time the lightning flashed, Jasmine saw the fear reflected in the eyes of her family. The crashes became louder and louder until it was absolutely deafening. In a sudden bright blaze Jasmine saw the great oak explode into millions of pieces and an angry fire engulf the remnants of the magnificent tree. As the river of water fell from the sky the fire soon became a smouldering heap with dense black smoke billowing in the fearless wind.

In all her years, Jasmine could never remember such a night. The fierce rain lashed at the squirrels as they cowered by the drey, forcing them further and further back into their home. Soon Jasmine was soaked, her fur dark and matted, water streaming into her ears and eyes.

Frantically she rubbed them clear, anxious to keep a careful watch for the dear tree that held their drey. If the tree was hit they would have to run for safety. And where could they go? She tried not to think of it. She kept herself alert to the sounds, the crashing and banging and screaming as the storm passed. Was the rain easing, or was it wishful thinking? But suddenly a blinding flash, a gigantic crack, and the very next tree keeled over, smashing to the ground and bursting open its heart below. Jasmine closed her eyes in horror. So close. She hoped the squirrels in that drey had had time to leave. If not......

Each moment seemed like an eternity as they sat silently watching and listening. Each could feel the other close by and took comfort from it. Jasmine's eyes ached and watered incessantly as she kept her constant vigil.

Gradually she realised that the periods of darkness were becoming longer and that the great, fierce lights in the sky were fading. Soon the wind eased and the rain began to fall gently, caressing the squirrels' fur and seeming for all the world like a gentle summer shower.

Quickly Jasmine and Chestnut raced to the ground to check that the squirrels in the stricken tree next door were safe and had shelter. They found the mother squirrel and her family emerging from the hollow bark of a nearby oak. They looked at each other with muted faces, and after a few brief words Jasmine and Chestnut returned to their tree. The homeless squirrel family were going to find their old drey which they had left in the spring. It was small, but safe, warm and dry.

With a sigh of relief Jasmine turned and hustled her family back inside the drey. Everyone suddenly stopped, and as Jasmine pushed her way to the front she could not help smiling. Despite the havoc and destruction outside, the deafening noise and the unceasing rain, Rowan lay curled up, fast asleep. He had slept through it all. Even when Ivy shook vigorously over him, purposely soaking him, he did not wake. Jasmine felt her heart go out to her youngest son.

'Sleep soundly, my son. Sleep soundly,' she whispered.

CHAPTER FIVE

The sun had risen and set for several days, and Rowan had remained close to the drey. The incident with the hawk had really frightened him, and he began to wonder what other horrors lay away from the safety of his home. He felt he needed to be near to the drey, to always be able to see it when he looked up. Just to know it was there.

Jasmine had talked to him for some time after the horror of the hawk attack. She had told him about the great flying birds, and about stoats, and also foxes. Rowan had been intrigued to learn that foxes had great bushy tails just like squirrels. But Jasmine told him some terrible stories about these foxes, so that he knew he must beware of them.

It seemed to Rowan that life was full of dangers. In addition to the new enemies he had learnt about, there were still the Grey Invaders. He thought of the times he had played at his secret place, never giving a thought to hawks, or stoats, or foxes. He shuddered. Now he was afraid to return there alone.

So it was that several days passed before Rowan could raise enough courage to go through the wood again. This time, instead of skipping and jumping along as before, he moved cautiously, peering this way and that, and darting frantically up the nearest tree whenever he heard a twig fall or a branch snap. By the time he reached the clearing his tail was bristling and his teeth were gnashing. His breath came in gulps and he ran to the stream and drank the cool water gratefully.

After quenching his thirst, he scampered up a nearby pine and had a good look around. There was no movement anywhere below him, and craning his neck he scoured the sky above. There were no hawks. He breathed a long sigh of relief and after another quick look below, hurried down the tree and began to run along beside the stream towards where he had met Fern.

As the stream widened he recognised the area at once. He looked around eagerly. No sign of her. He began to sniff the ground by the bank hoping to find a sign that she had been there recently. Backwards and forwards he ran, sniffing and snuffling as he went. He came across a few half-chewed acorns and examined them carefully. There was a strange smell about them, but he could not identify it.

Thoughtfully he looked at the expanse of water before him. What he really ought to do was to swim across to the other side. Rowan knew that might take him dangerously close to Grey Squirrel Island, but he was anxious to find his new friend. So taking a deep breath, he plunged into the cool water and swam swiftly to the other side. No playing or splashing this time. As soon as he reached the bank, he pulled himself out and shook vigorously, quickly looking upwards to make sure no black shadow was lurking.

The whole area on this side of the stream smelled strange, like a musty drey on a damp morning. He began to regret his impulsive decision to swim over alone.

Suddenly there was a growl behind him. Without even looking back, Rowan jumped into a nearby tree and climbed as fast as he could to the very top. He clung tightly to the branches as his body shook with fear. His heart pounded like the thunder in the storm.

From below him came a giggle, and a snort, and another giggle.

'My, my. We are jumpy today.'

Rowan froze. Which enemy was this? Was it a stoat pretending to sound like another squirrel, or was it a hawk, trying to fool him again?

'Are you going to stay up there all day?' came the voice again. Rowan edged along to the end of the branch in an attempt to see who was speaking to him.

'Well, you're not being very friendly at all. First of all you say you'll meet me, and then you don't bother to turn up for days. I don't know why I'm even bothering to talk to you.'

By now Rowan was hanging upside down, trying to see the animal below. He leaned further and further forward until, finally, he could see her.

Feeling rather silly, he tried to climb down the tree with as much dignity as possible, and when he was halfway down jumped spectacularly, tumbling over and over on the ground and landing in a heap at Fern's feet.

She stepped back in amazement. 'You certainly are the strangest squirrel I have ever met. Are all red squirrels like you?'

Rowan sat down and began to groom nonchalantly. 'I was just checking that it was all clear.'

'What were you expecting?' asked Fern, confused by his strange behaviour.

'Well,' replied Rowan matter-of-factly, 'you just never know, do you? Could be stoats, foxes, hawks...'

Fern gasped. 'Not here, surely?' she whispered, looking around fearfully. Rowan saw that she was afraid and moved closer to her.

'Don't worry,' he said softly, 'I've had a good look round. It's definitely safe here.' Fern looked relieved.

'I'm glad you came.' she said, moving over to a group of young saplings. 'Come over here and see what I've found.'

Rowan hurried over to her and was pleased to see several succulent pine cones and fresh, green acorns, gathered together in a tidy pile. Together they sat and ate noisily, relishing the tasty pine seeds, holding them in their paws and tearing at the scales with their teeth. Neither spoke. Every now and then one or the other would skip over to the stream and have a drink, then return and chew vigorously again.

When they had finished eating they both lay down under the shade of the saplings and rested. Quietly, Fern asked,

'Why did you take so long to come back?'

Rowan paused for a moment and then began to tell her about the hawk's attack. Fern listened carefully, occasionally squealing with horror. He told her how the huge bird had spoken to him and how he had been unable to move, how Juniper had run to him, risking his own life, and that by biting behind his ear his brother had saved his life. He told her how the hawk had shouted and screamed at the family and explained that he had been too frightened to venture far away from the drey.

Fern said she quite understood, and thought Rowan terribly brave to come at all.

'Nonsense,' said Rowan shyly, 'I wanted to see you again.'

Fern looked pleased and tossed her head coyly. 'I'm glad you came,' she murmured.

Feeling content and full after their feast they settled down into the lush grass and soft leaves below the tiny trees. Lying close together they fell asleep in the early evening warmth.

Some time later Rowan awoke feeling stiff and cold. He was surprised to find his coat damp, and the ground around him sparkling with water droplets. It had begun to rain.

Fern was awake now. She shook herself thoroughly and quickly smoothed down her coat and preened her tail. The rain started to fall heavily and the saplings were giving little shelter.

'I must go now,' said Fern, heading off into the undergrowth. She turned briefly and called goodbye, and then hurried away.

Rowan looked at the stream and thought how uninviting it looked now. Taking a deep breath he jumped into the water and swam swiftly to the other side. Quickly he hurried into the woods, heading for home. Although he was wet and cold, he felt wonderful. He had so enjoyed Fern's company and could not wait until tomorrow when he could return again. Then he stopped, realising they had said nothing about another meeting. He turned, hesitating. He was far into the wood now, and did not know which way Fern had gone. Looking up at the growing darkness he decided to continue on his way home. He was sure she would be there tomorrow.

Rowan was completely soaked and had to keep stopping to shake the excess water from his coat. It was getting darker and darker and the falling raindrops were making strange noises on the leaves. In fact he noticed there were strange noises all round. He began to run as fast as he could, knowing that he must not stop again. If it became completely dark he would not be able to find his way back to the drey. He had never been away from home for so long before, and began to feel frightened. Thankfully the end of the wood was near, and soon he was galloping up the hill to the home trees. As familiar faces and sounds and sights appeared he began to slow down. Friends called to him and chattered as he passed, and he was reassured by the scurrying and hurrying of the busy wood as other squirrels returned to their dreys for the night.

There was a snort from behind, and a sharp prick on his back. Jumping into the air with surprise, Rowan turned to see Juniper, winking at him mischievously.

'Oh, Juniper,' he said with relief, 'you startled me.'

'You'll be more than startled when you get back to the drey,' replied Juniper, trotting beside his brother. 'Mother is furious you have stayed out so late. She sent Chestnut and me to look for you.'

'Oh dear,' sighed Rowan.

'Where have you been?' queried Juniper.

Rowan did not reply. Juniper became impatient. 'Oh, come on, it's only fair to tell me. I'm tired out, you know. I've been out all day with Chestnut restocking with food and we're exhausted. He's not too pleased, let me tell you, having to turn round and come out again to look for you.'

By this time they had reached the drey and Rowan thankfully climbed the home tree, desperately trying to think of a good reason for being late. He was reluctant to lie to his mother again, but was also anxious not to let anyone know about his secret place.

Jasmine was waiting for him, but when she saw her wet and bedraggled son her anger evaporated. She made him shake himself again and again and then she, Ivy and Petal all groomed him meticulously until he was dry and warm again. She was not sure that she believed his explanation that he had fallen asleep in the rain, but all that mattered was that he was home and safe.

Jasmine felt fortunate that she still had all her family with her. She knew it would not be long before Chestnut and Juniper left, and Ivy and Petal moved to new dreys to have their own infants. She thought again of the incident with the hawk, and shuddered. Nudging gently into the centre of the drey, she slept contentedly with her family around her.

CHAPTER SIX

Chestnut, Juniper and Rowan were sitting beneath the home tree enjoying the sunshine. Juniper had once again been persuaded to distribute some of his secret store of pine cones, but in return Chestnut had produced some green acorns and Rowan had collected a few young, fresh, sweet-chestnut leaves. They were beginning some friendly bartering when there was a sudden commotion a short distance away. They watched in surprise as two squirrels came racing through the trees, ears flattened and eyes bright with fear. Chestnut recognised them and called out loudly,

'Burdock! Dandelion! What on earth is the matter?'

At first they did not seem to hear him, but then the first squirrel turned his head and seeing the familiar group of faces swerved and almost crashed into Juniper and Rowan. The second squirrel reluctantly halted and joined them.

'What is it?' asked Chestnut again, but neither could reply. Their sides were heaving and their mouths drooling as they sobbed and wailed. Soon several other squirrels, attracted by the strange noises, joined them until quite a large group had formed around the distraught pair. After a while Dandelion began to recover, and in a voice that quivered as he spoke, started to explain.

'We were bored....' he said looking around miserably at his friends and neighbours, all anxious and concerned, every eye watching and waiting. 'Very bored, in fact. And Parsley suggested we go exploring. He said he had been to the bottom of the hill and he wanted to see what lay beyond.'

There were gasps from the onlookers.

Dandelion nodded, 'I know we should not have gone, but it seemed a good idea at the time.'

'I wanted to turn back as soon as we found the dead pigeon,' shouted Burdock, still shaking and shivering. Dandelion looked at him harshly and continued,

'Anyway, as Burdock said, we came across this dead bird. We thought it was sleeping at first, but then we smelt it.'

'It had a great gaping hole in its side,' cried Burdock, ignoring the withering look from Dandelion.

More gulps and exclamations from the crowd.

'As I was saying, yes it was dead, and there was a dreadful smell of fear about it. Burdock wanted to come home but Parsley kept saying it wasn't far and we should keep going.'

'Where is Parsley?' quizzed Chestnut.

Burdock began to babble then, and Dandelion choked and stuttered. Every squirrel watching became totally still and silent.

'We came to a place where there were no trees,' continued Dandelion, 'so we had to run as fast as we could. There was no shelter for us and we were really frightened. If there had been a hawk, we would have been done for.'

'Tell them about the big bird,' urged Burdock. Dandelion nodded.

'While we were running this huge bird flew up from the ground in front of us, squawking and yelling at us. It was much bigger than a hawk, and was really clumsy. It was so big it could hardly fly. We thought it was going to attack us, but it just hurried away from us making this terrible noise.'

'A pheasant,' declared Chestnut. The others nodded mutely.

'Tell them, go on. Tell them,' cried Burdock, his voice rising to a high pitch.

'Come on,' said Chestnut, becoming alarmed. Tears began to trickle down his cheeks as Dandelion completed his story.

'When the.......pheasant.........had gone we came to a bank, and then a strange place. The ground was hard and uncomfortable and hurt our feet, and there was something black and horrible on it that felt sticky when we touched it. Burdock and I stood at the edge smelling it. We were afraid to walk on it, but Parsley was standing right in the middle of it. He was really excited and jumping up and down and saying there was another wood and we were just about to follow him when.....' Dandelion hesitated, 'when there was a terrible noise and a huge monster came roaring round the corner. It was shiny and had two great eyes at the front and a huge silver mouth, and as it passed us its breath knocked us over. It made a horrible grinding noise and as I looked up I saw something inside it. It had a big head and was sitting inside the monster, as if it was telling the monster where to go. As it left there was a big cloud of black smoke behind it.'

'Tell them. Tell them,' moaned Burdock.

'All *right*. Well, then we looked for Parsley, but we couldn't see him at first. We called to him, and then Burdock saw him lying on the black stuff. He was dead. The monster had killed him.'

A huge monster

There were wails from the listening females, Burdock began to sob again, and Dandelion hung his head low.

Jasmine had been sitting away from the others, quietly waiting for Dandelion to finish. Now she came forward and sat beside the two forlorn squirrels.

'It was a human's machine,' she declared. There were a few murmurings from some of the older squirrels present, but most of the youngsters were confused and began asking questions.

'What's a human?' asked one. 'What's a machine?' asked another. Jasmine hushed them.

'Be quiet and I'll tell you. I suppose you could say that a human is a type of animal. They walk on two legs, not four like us. Don't worry, they don't live here on Tolls Hill. Their dreys are called houses and they are made of stone. They are not so fast at running or climbing as squirrels, and so they sometimes have machines that carry them around. That was what killed Parsley.'

Jasmine sighed and looked around her. Everyone was listening intently.

'So you see, that is why you must never go away from the hill, because if the humans in their machines don't get you, the hawks or the foxes will.'

There was consternation among the gathering. Hardly anyone ever spoke about leaving the hill. Why should they want to? Certainly not now they knew what was out there.

Jasmine began to shoo the others away. 'Go on now, all go home. Burdock and Dandelion, come with me to see Parsley's family to explain to them.'

Rowan watched them leave and began to tremble. Once again he began to wonder if he ought to tell someone about his secret place. More importantly, was it safe to go there at all?

He had arranged to meet Fern later that day, but instead curled up inside the drey and slept. Occasionally he could be heard to murmur 'Tuk. Tuk. Tuk.'

It was a time of long, hot, lazy days when the sunshine glistened on the dew-laden leaves, bees hunted busily for nectar, butterflies floated on the breeze, and the sweet smell of summer flowers filled the air. Eventually Rowan had overcome his fear and had returned to his secret place, and now met Fern regularly by the stream. Rowan looked forward to their meetings. They would look for food together, sharing treasured finds of pine cones, tender young shoots, and even an occasional mushroom or toadstool. Rowan had pulled a strange face at first, but with Fern's tender coaxing had grown to like the strange food. Fern had explained that mushrooms were a special treat to the inhabitants of Grey Squirrel Island.

Now this was a topic of conversation that Rowan loved to hear about - the other squirrel island. Sometimes, Fern would be strangely silent and refuse to discuss her home life. Other times Rowan would listen enthralled by the stories she had to tell of her home. He carefully noted all the references made to Scarface and Thistle, although these were few. She seemed almost afraid to mention their names. There were others like Ragwort and Nettle. Rowan soon realised that not only Fern, but most of the other squirrels on Grey Squirrel Island were afraid of them. They were patrollers, Fern explained, and worked on orders from Scarface.

Rowan soon noticed that Fern became agitated and nervous when talking about these ferocious squirrels. He collected the little information that he could now and then, building up a picture of giant silver animals with razor-sharp teeth and deadly claws. Often he would recall his dream of the giant acorn, and shudder.

Fern had listened politely to his story of the dream. Not once had she laughed or scorned him for his fear. They had discussed the possibility of there being such an acorn. It was so nice to have such a friend to discuss these things with, someone who would not laugh and call him silly and young, as some squirrels did.

One particularly hot day, Rowan was ambling through the wood on his way to meet Fern. He was very hot and thirsty, and as soon as he heard the water, he began to hurry, until he was racing along excitedly. Without pausing for breath, he tore through the grass and plunged headlong into the water. It felt so good. He dived and swam, and splashed and blew bubbles.

'Come on Fern,' he thought impatiently, 'do hurry up and join me.' He continued splashing and playing until he began to grow tired, then took a final dive and swam under the water to the other bank. Pulling himself on to the grass he lay panting in the sunshine, his body dripping, the water from his fur making little pools beside him.

As he began to recover he shook and shook until his coat was almost dry. He looked in the direction of Grey Squirrel Island. Fern was late today. Whenever he heard a rustle he looked up expectantly, but it was only the wind blowing through the trees.

He started to forage but did not feel hungry. He was worried. Why was she so late?

After a while he could stand the waiting no longer. The sun was high overhead. Rowan knew that something must be wrong. He scampered quickly up a nearby tree and gazed towards Fern's home. There was no movement. He jumped across to another tree, and another, and another. Still there was no sign of her.

Perched as high up the tree as he could get, Rowan looked back towards the stream. He had already moved some way from it. He looked around carefully, trying to memorise all the trees, saplings and hills. He knew that he would have to go to Grey Squirrel Island to meet Fern. He knew he had to go now, and alone.

Taking a deep breath, he jumped down the tree and began to move away from the familiar sound of the stream in the direction that he had often seen Fern travel. Behind him the familiar sound of the water grew more and more distant, and he became aware of new smells around him. His teeth began to chatter and the bristles on his tail were standing on end, but he plunged forward, determined to find his friend.

There were strange moaning sounds in this wood, almost as if the very trees were calling to him. Rowan tried not to listen to them, thinking only of finding Fern. Soon the leaves on the trees became so thick that they cloaked the wood in darkness. He climbed a large tree nearby, moving right up to the top until he could see both the way he had come and the way he was going. He jumped from one tree-top to another, until he saw a small clearing below. Then he ran and slithered his way down. Almost immediately he noticed strange markings on the turf. He sniffed around carefully. He was so engrossed in this new find that at first he did not hear the distant chattering and snorting. It became louder and louder until Rowan realised it was not merely his heart pounding. The noises were very near. Very frightened, he darted into a thicket, not noticing the thorns and the sharp branches as they scraped his back and legs.

There was a terrible noise nearby. A squirrel shrieked, then another. Then he heard growls and squeals and a high, piercing wail. Rowan could not move. He was horrified by the noises that he heard. Frantically he glanced around. Nothing moved, but the sounds seemed to be so close.

His first instinct was to turn and run back the way he had come, but he struggled against his fear, determined to find out what was happening in this strange place. Taking a deep breath he crept slowly forward. The commotion was just the other side of the next tree. He lay on his stomach and crawled along the ground, at the same time looking in every direction. As he approached the tree he suddenly made a dash for it, ran madly up the trunk and into the shelter of the branches. The leaves were so thick he could see very little, and so he moved further up the tree in an effort to see better.

The noise from below was growing louder and louder, and then Rowan knew what the sound was. It was the chattering and grinding of squirrels' teeth. Sounds that squirrels who were frightened and fearful made. He edged himself further and further along the branch until there, below, he saw the awful scene. The whole area was a mass of grey squirrels. They stood in groups, shivering and shaking. In the centre stood a large, silver animal who raised his head in the air and spoke to them. His claws glistened in the sunlight and his tail was so bushy it was almost as big as his body.

'He must be the leader,' thought Rowan. He turned his head slightly, and Rowan jumped back in alarm as he saw the jagged, ugly scar on the side of his face.

'Scarface!' squealed Rowan.

Rowan looked around him quickly and saw that the next tree would give him a much better view, and would also enable him to listen to what was said. With a tremendous effort he launched himself through the air and landed safely in the boughs of the tree. He froze as the tree shook and several of the grey squirrels looked around them. It seemed as if they were looking right at him and Rowan was sure his shaking claws would lose their grip on the branch and he would fall and land right in the middle of the crowd of squirrels.

After a short while when nothing had happened he eased himself into a comfortable position and then settled down to listen. The giant grey squirrel, whom Rowan now knew to be Scarface, was shouting to the other squirrels.

'...and this stupid, ignorant squirrel has the audacity to stand here and say she is sorry.' Much discussion amongst the onlookers. 'Sorry, is she? I'll make her sorry. Come and stand before me, traitor.'

Scarface nodded to two nearby squirrels who disappeared briefly and then returned with a writhing, squealing, tiny grey female. Rowan gasped, horrified.... It was Fern!

She was dragged before Scarface who, facing her, struck her savagely across the head, his claws tearing her forehead. Blood began to pour from the wound. Fern cried out with the pain.

Rowan gripped tightly on to the branch, willing himself to keep still. He longed to race down and save Fern, but he knew that he would not have a chance. He needed time to think of a plan. He leaned precariously over the branch to listen.

Scarface moved up close to the cowering female, sneering at her from behind the ghastly scar.

'Well,' he yelled, pushing his nose cruelly against her face, 'what have you got to say?'

She started to back away from him, the blood running down her face and dripping on to the ground. She was so frightened she could not answer.

'Well?' he thundered.

'I'm s-s-sorry,' she mumbled.

'You're sorry, are you?' Scarface screamed at her.

Fern wiped the blood away from her eyes and looked sorrowfully at him. 'I didn't know it was wrong,' she whispered.

Scarface laughed loudly, and the two squirrels who had fetched her laughed with him. He did not notice that the others were silent. Suddenly he jumped into the air and then stood proudly on his hind legs, towering above them all. He put his head back and shrilled a loud, terrible howl. Rowan was shaking so much he had difficulty in keeping his balance in the tree.

Scarface then began pacing around Fern, who was by now shaking uncontrollably. He was obviously enjoying himself immensely and was determined to make the most of it.

'You didn't know it was wrong,' he hissed, 'not wrong to associate with a RED SQUIRREL!' he yelled excitedly. Again murmurings and rumblings from the others. He began to dance and jump about, screaming at her as she cringed lower and lower.

Rowan did not know whether to stay and see what would happen or to run home as quickly as he could and get help. Would the others believe him? Would they help Fern?

'Oh, I wish Chestnut was here,' he thought desperately. Below, Scarface and his two helpers, who Rowan realised must be Ragwort and Nettle, were moving amongst the other squirrels, inciting them to scream and shriek. Soon the air was filled with chanting. 'TRAITOR. TRAITOR.'

The tree was shaking with the noise, and Rowan wedged himself firmly between two thick branches, hoping that he would not fall out and land at the feet of Scarface.

Suddenly it went quiet below. There was hissing and shushing, and a loud *'Be still.'* Scarface stood up again and looked down upon the others.

'It is simple. She must die,' he declared, enjoying the looks of horror on the squirrels' faces. There were gasps. Fern collapsed. Scarface looked at Ragwort and Nettle, and they began to chant. 'DIE. DIE.'

However, they soon stopped. No squirrel took up the chant with them. It was then that there was a movement from within the crowd. The squirrels moved aside as a large, beautiful silver squirrel stepped forward.

'What do you want, Thistle?' said Scarface sneeringly.

Thistle looked towards the terrified Fern and then moved closer to Scarface. The two stood glaring at each other, their tails flapping angrily. Finally Scarface looked away, and Thistle turned to speak to the others.

'We do not take the life of our own without a trial,' he said, looking fiercely towards Scarface. There were murmurings of agreement as Thistle continued. 'If this young female is found guilty of associating with a red squirrel, then she must be punished.'

'Yes. Punished,' shouted Ragwort and Nettle together, but they looked away quickly as Thistle glared at them.

'When the sun rises again, we shall hear her story,' he continued. Then he looked at two squirrels nearby and went up to them.

'Take her away and keep her safe,' he looked around him, 'and we will meet here again with the new sun.' Then he left, and the crowd began to disperse.

Scarface was furious and motioned to Ragwort and Nettle to join him. They muttered secretly, and Rowan, try as he might, could not hear them.

Rowan watched as Fern was led away. He was relieved to see the two jailors treat her gently. She was brought very near to the tree that he was hiding in and was suddenly afraid that a drey might be concealed near him. He was very surprised to see her led into a hole in the ground. It looked very much like an old rabbit burrow.

'At least I know where she is,' thought Rowan, 'I must get home and tell the others.'

Determined to save his friend, he hurried down the tree and back in the direction of the stream. The birds and rabbits looked on in amazement as the red squirrel moved swiftly past them. A hawk flying overhead decided that the animal was moving too fast even for him to catch.

Rowan did not pause once to catch his breath. Already a plan was forming in his mind. He was anxious to reach home as quickly as possible to discuss it with Chestnut and Juniper.

CHAPTER SEVEN

There was a large gathering on Tolls Hill. Jasmine had summoned all the squirrels to an emergency meeting. They sat in their family groups and listened to the story that Rowan told.

Rowan was surprised that there had been no reproaches. Jasmine was as concerned for Fern as if she were one of her own children.

All were horrified at what they heard, and there was much grinding and gnashing of teeth amongst the younger squirrels. Jasmine stepped forward and scanned the crowd before her.

'Redfox,' she called, searching the faces. 'If you are here, we need your help.'

Rowan looked at his mother in surprise. Whoever was Redfox? He had never heard the name before. Even Juniper and Chestnut looked at each other in bewilderment. Then from the masses stepped a large squirrel, striking in his appearance. His coat gleamed bright red, far redder than any other, and his tail was long and bushy. The sunlight seemed to make him glow. His eyes were bright and sparkling and the plumes on his ears were magnificent.

'Yes,' he replied in a clear voice, 'I am here.'

Jasmine and Redfox touched noses and then Jasmine backed away. Rowan watched in awe as the animal before him looked slowly around, scrutinising each face. When his eyes found Rowan, they stopped.

'Ah,' he beamed, moving towards him, 'so you are the bearer of these ill-tidings, are you?'

Rowan cowered low and looked pleadingly towards Jasmine. To his surprise, she twitched her whiskers and winked at him. Redfox now stood before him.

'Now, Rowan,' he said softly, 'I want you to tell me everything that you can remember about Grey Squirrel Island.'

'No!' whispered Rowan. There were gasps of amazement from all around.

'What did you say?' asked Redfox.

Rowan gulped. He was desperately trying to stop his teeth from chattering and his tail from quivering. He took a deep breath.

'I cannot,' he said, raising himself from the ground and sitting erect before Redfox. He continued, 'I don't mean to be rude, but there is no more time. We must all rush back to the island, invade it, and save Fern.'

Redfox squatted so that his eyes were level with Rowan's face. 'Oh, I see,' his ears began to twitch as he smiled, 'Of course we will do all we can to save your friend, but we must have a plan of action, my dear, young, impulsive and brave Rowan.' He moved forward and rubbed Rowan's cheek with his nose.

'A plan?' enquired Rowan.

'Yes,' said Redfox, gazing around him. 'I want all the adult males to gather round, and listen again carefully to what Rowan has to say.'

Many squirrels now came forward and positioned themselves around this magnificent stranger. No one thought to question his authority. He was without doubt their leader.

'Now, Rowan. How many males were there, do you think?'

'I couldn't tell,' he replied. 'There was Scarface and Thistle, and Ragwort and Nettle, and several others who I think were patrollers.'

'How many other squirrels were there?' asked Redfox.

Rowan thought carefully for a moment. 'At least as many as there are here. Probably more.'

One of the squirrels moved forward. The others looked at him expectantly. This was another newcomer. A squirrel who had only recently joined them on Tolls Hill and who as yet had spoken only to a few.

'If I may be permitted to speak?' he asked, addressing Redfox.

'I'm sorry, we have not met before?'

'No,' replied the newcomer. 'My name is Moss, and I come from a wood that lies beyond the next hill. I may be able to help you. You see, I have been to Grey Squirrel Island.'

'When?' asked Redfox.

'Not long ago, my home also was attacked by grey squirrels.

I had lived there all my life, and I had a homely drey, with my female, and five infants. The hill was a happy place, and our only danger was from a family of stoats that lived at the bottom of the wood nearby. That was why we called it Stoat Hill. Anyway, one day we males were out foraging and we heard terrible squeals and howlings. I thought it was the stoats, and raced back to the drey. Several of us had been quite a way away, where we had found a horde of fallen pine cones, so it took us a while to get back.'

Moss sighed, and the other squirrels drew closer as they listened.

'All I could see were silver streaks. There were grey squirrels everywhere. They had killed my family and all the other females and infants. I was so angry. I saw a grey squirrel running down the hill, and I followed him. I wanted to kill him. He was moving fast and I was tiring. My anger made me carry on. We ran and ran for such a long time; my legs hurt and my head was pounding. I knew that I must catch the murderer and kill him. I was nearly on him, when I heard a commotion nearby. I did not know what to do, so I climbed up a nearby tree. A crowd of grey squirrels were returning, laughing and snorting together. They were covered in blood. The blood of my friends and family. I was shaking with rage and despair. I followed them until they reached their home. Their females came to greet them. I heard the squirrel I had been chasing proudly boasting to his infants that he had killed six red squirrels.'

Rowan moaned impatiently. He began to pace restlessly backwards and forwards. There were whispers around him. Moss paused momentarily. Redfox glared at Rowan and then moved beside Moss and nudged him gently.

'Please go on. We haven't got much time,' he whispered. Moss nodded, and continued.

'It looked as if the red squirrels had put up a brave fight in protecting their infants, for some of the returning greys were wounded and bleeding. They were so big and powerful. The reds couldn't have stood a chance. I continued watching for a while until I saw the squirrel I had been chasing amble off to a nearby stream to wash his wounds. It was then I took my chance. Not caring whether I was caught or not, I followed him to the stream and pounced on him. There was a fight and I killed him. He died quickly and quietly so no-one heard. Then I left. After days of wandering in the wood, I came to Tolls Hill.'

'But what do you know about Grey Squirrel Island?' asked Rowan impatiently. Moss nodded thoughtfully.

'I know the best route to get there, where the dreys are, and where the guards are positioned.'

He looked around him. 'I am so grateful to you for accepting me into your territory when I had no home or family. Maybe I can repay you by helping to destroy the grey squirrels.'

'The Grey Invaders,' said Rowan, stepping forward.

'Yes,' declared Redfox, 'the Grey Invaders. We must defeat them once and for all.'

Rowan was becoming very anxious. They had been talking for such a long time, and still there was no plan for Fern's escape. Frantically, Rowan nudged Juniper away from the others.

'What is it?' asked Juniper, rather annoyed that he was missing the important meeting. Rowan's teeth were chattering and his tail jerking uncontrollably. Juniper sighed. His brother was so excitable. Whatever could be upsetting him now?

'Calm down, Rowan. For goodness' sake. How can I help you if you don't tell me what is wrong?'

Rowan tried to collect himself, and in a tight voice said 'Fern. What about Fern?'

Juniper was exasperated. 'That's what we're trying to decide now,' he hissed, and began to move back towards the meeting. Rowan quickly moved in front of him, blocking his path.

'Please Juniper,' he whispered urgently, 'please listen to me.'

Juniper glanced at the others, and then sat down. 'Go on, then,' he sighed, 'but make it short.'

Rowan sat down beside his brother and looked towards the gathering nearby.

'It will be dark soon, and then no one will dare go off the hill. By the time tomorrow comes it will be too late. They will kill her.'

Juniper thought hard about what his brother had said. He was right, of course. He looked at the sky. The sun was already setting and the first hints of grey could be seen in the distance. He turned to his brother. 'I'll go and speak to them. Perhaps we can devise a plan.'

Rowan jumped up. 'No. That's no good. They've been doing that all afternoon. We've got to go by ourselves. Please help me, Juniper, please,' he said, pleading with his brother.

Juniper looked at him and saw the tears in his eyes.

'Please will you help me?' asked Rowan imploringly.

'On our own?' asked Juniper.

Rowan talked quickly. 'We must. There is no time to lose. I can show you where she is. You can create a diversion, and...'

Juniper whispered hoarsely, 'Me? Create a diversion? How?'

'We'll think of that when we get there.'

'Oh, that's a marvellous plan,' said Juniper with contempt.

'Shush,' Rowan said quickly. 'Anyway, you create a diversion and I will go down into the rabbit hole and find her. Then we can race back here in time to join the others when they invade Grey Squirrel Island.'

Rowan was pleased with himself. It sounded so straight-forward. What a hero he would be when he returned with Fern. He noticed the frown on his brother's face. He was not convinced.

'Quickly, Juniper. Let's go now. Come on.' Rowan hurried away, anxious that Juniper should not let him down by refusing to go. 'Come on. Come *on*,' he called.

Oh well, it might just work, thought Juniper, and he gave a deep sigh, and followed Rowan into the shadow of the wood.

CHAPTER EIGHT

Juniper was muttering to himself. He knew he should not have followed his crazy brother. Here they were, in a strange wood with great, menacing trees and peculiar sounds and even stranger smells. He had no idea where they were and doubted that Rowan did either. He seemed to know where he was going, but Juniper was not so sure.

Every now and then Rowan paused to sniff around, and his whiskers jerked and his hackles rose with every noise. Rowan was galloping on ahead, and Juniper was anxious not to lose sight of him. 'That's all I need,' he thought, 'to have to rescue both of them.'

Suddenly Rowan stopped and Juniper, in his hurry, ran right into him. They tumbled over each other and Rowan had difficulty in keeping Juniper quiet. After they had both calmed down, they could hear soft snortings and growlings nearby. In a flash they both hurried up a tree and climbed right to the top until they could see what was happening. Juniper's teeth began to grind and Rowan hissed at him to be quiet. Juniper closed his mouth and hoped that no one could hear the pounding of his heart.

Carefully they peered out. There were the grey squirrels, just as Rowan had left them. Some were now quietly asleep, others sat together in little groups, discussing the day. Juniper's eyes grew larger and larger as he scanned the vast army of faces below him.

'Oh my word,' stammered Juniper.

Rowan was next to him, whispering. 'What?' then sucked in his breath quickly when he realised he had spoken out loud.

'There must be hundreds of them.'

Rowan gave him a darting look. 'There. You see those two grey squirrels by the rabbit hole, just at the bottom of that tall pine tree?'

Juniper followed the direction of his brother's eyes and then saw the hole. He nodded.

'They took her in there.' Juniper gulped. There were grey

squirrels everywhere. In fact, the ground was a mass of silver shadows. If one of them looked up and saw them....

The branch began to shake and quiver and Rowan was terrified to see Juniper struggling to hold on. Quickly he grabbed his brother by the neck, just in time to save him from falling at the feet of the squirrels.

'It's alright,' whispered Rowan, 'I nearly fell out of the tree when I first saw them. You'll calm down in a minute.'

'That's good to know.'

Gradually the wobbling branch settled, and Juniper was able to gulp back his fear. The two red squirrels sat side by side, looking at the scene before them. Suddenly, Juniper grew excited.

'I've got it,' he exclaimed, and Rowan immediately glared at him. 'I've got it,' he whispered urgently.

'Well?' enquired Rowan.

Juniper moved in as close as he could get without actually sitting on top of his brother.

'You see that big broken branch over there.' Rowan looked, and nodded. 'Well if I gnaw at it until it falls, the noise it would make would distract the grey squirrels, and you could rush in and get your friend.'

'Brilliant!' said Rowan. Juniper was pleased that he had thought of such a good plan. He would be the hero when they returned.

'You get over to the branch and get to work, and I'll get in as close as I can without being seen.'

Juniper nodded, and scampered away. Rowan took a deep breath and then hurried down the tree and moved stealthily closer to the Grey Invaders. Soon he was only a whisker away, and could smell the strange, different scent of the creatures.

Juniper was busily gnawing and grinding at the branch. He knew he had to hurry and kept looking quickly in Rowan's direction. He coughed and spluttered as a piece of dry wood stuck to the roof of his mouth. He spat it out loudly. Then he coughed again. Suddenly there was a growl below. Instantly he froze. Another growl. Slowly Juniper looked below. There sat a huge grey squirrel watching him, a menacing look in his eyes. Juniper stifled a scream. He looked towards Rowan, who was watching in horror. What should he do?

With teeth bared the grey squirrel launched himself at Juniper. Rowan watched in alarm as the huge squirrel landed on the branch in front of his brother. Juniper's eyes rolled as the grey glared at him.

Suddenly there was a loud crack and the branch snapped at the point where Juniper had been gnawing. The grey squirrel fell heavily, the broken branch landing on his head. He lay motionless. Rowan crept cautiously to the body. It did not move. He could hear Juniper's teeth chattering. He sniffed carefully.

'He's dead,' he whispered urgently. 'Juniper. Did you hear me? He's dead. It's alright.' Juniper nodded.

'What shall we do now?'

Rowan thought for a moment. 'You'll just have to yell, or throw something. I don't know. You'll have to think of an idea.'

'Me?'

'Yes. Come on Juniper, you can do it. I must get on,' Rowan whispered as he ran back towards the guards. Rowan tried to ignore the worried look on his brother's face.

He was soon close enough to hear the two guards laughing and talking together.

'It will be a good day,' said one.

'The best,' said the other. A snigger.

'I bet she'll die screaming,' said the first again.

Rowan longed to plunge forward and sink his teeth into the guard's neck. Then he heard a whispering. Fern.

The second guard poked his head into the rabbit hole. 'Shut up, traitor,' and the noise stopped.

'Stupid squirrel,' he hissed.

Rowan was so angry he trembled with rage. Just at that moment there was a loud screech and loud yelling.

'Yah! Yah! Silly old squirrels. Yah! Yah!'

After a moment Rowan recognised his brother's voice and smiled. 'Well done, Juniper,' he thought.

Several of the larger male grey squirrels hurried to investigate, including the two guards. Without a moment to lose, Rowan darted forward and plunged into the hole. Down into the darkness he ran until he saw two luminous eyes before him. He stopped within inches of them.

'It's alright, Fern. It's me. Rowan,' he whispered urgently. There was no recognition in the frightened eyes. Rowan moved closer and nudged her gently. 'Fern. It's Rowan.'

A look of horror came into her eyes. 'Go away,' she cried.

Rowan could hear the commotion overhead. Every second counted. The guards would soon return. Closing his eyes, he bit her firmly. She squealed.

'Fern!' he hissed.

She blinked carefully, and then began to sniff at his coat. 'Rowan?'

With relief, he began to hurry back to the entrance. 'Quickly Fern. Follow me.'

She had not moved. 'Rowan?' she asked again.

Exasperated, expecting at any minute to hear the guards returning, he turned and ran back to her and nudged her roughly.

'Quickly, you must come with me. There's no time to lose. I am here to save you.'

Confused, she slowly followed him. It seemed to Rowan that each step took an eternity.

In fact it had only taken a short while. By the time they reached daylight the guards were still cautiously investigating the strange noises. They had also now found the fallen branch and their dead companion. The brightness seemed to bring Fern to her senses, and she looked around her in amazement.

'Rowan. What's going on?'

'It's a diversion,' he whispered. 'We must run for our lives. Are you ready?'

'Yes.'

'We will meet my brother in the wood. Don't be afraid. Ready? Now. Run.'

Without looking either way they dashed across the short

clearing and into the wood. They ran and ran. Their breathing became harder and their lungs hurt but still they ran. Trees rushed past and their feet almost flew over the undergrowth.

Suddenly in front of them stood a red squirrel. Fern shrieked. Juniper looked at her in surprise.

'Is this....?' he began.

Without replying, Rowan ran on, closely followed by Fern. Juniper shrugged and then quickly joined them. Together they raced through the bracken and brambles, darting round towering trees and racing through grassy clearings. Rowan could see that Fern was slowing down. He tried to urge her on.

'Come on, Fern. You must hurry. They will soon find you've gone, and then come looking for you.'

He paused, waiting for her to catch up. Juniper was close by. They both noticed the blood on her feet. She was limping badly and was obviously in considerable pain.

'Fern. Your paws,' cried Rowan.

She came to a halt and looked at her wounds sorrowfully. 'They bit my foot,' she said miserably, 'to try to stop me running away.'

Rowan was crestfallen. 'Can you carry on?'

Fern sobbed. 'I'll try.'

'Let her rest for a moment,' said Juniper, and motioned for Rowan to follow him. They moved a little away from her. Juniper showed Rowan the trail of blood that Fern had left behind her.

'They will easily find us,' he said with concern. Rowan agreed. What else could they do?

Just then there was a rustle in the bush before them. Out jumped an enormous rabbit. It rose up from the ground on its massive hind legs and towered menacingly over them.

Both Rowan and Juniper were speechless, and Fern lay close to the ground trembling.

'Now look here,' said the rabbit, 'I am absolutely fed up with you squirrels disturbing the peace in my wood. First of all you...' he glared at Rowan, 'you come skipping into the forest, singing away, and completely out of tune, I might add. Then you splash and squeal in my stream. Then this grey squirrel joins you, and you both shout and splash and giggle all day long.' He looked at them hard. 'And now there are three of you, tearing around like a fox was after you. I've had enough, I tell you.'

With that he dropped on to all fours, and began to scratch behind his ear. The three squirrels were speechless. Having finished his scratch, the rabbit continued.

'Furthermore, judging by the commotion behind you I would say something is amiss. Is it anything to do with you, young lady?' he demanded, shoving his nose hard up against Fern's face. She cringed even lower. Rowan hesitated, then stepped forward, much to Juniper's horror.

'If this is your wood, Sir, then I am sorry that we have disturbed you. We are on a very important mission, and must leave now.' He began slowly to edge towards Fern. 'If our swimming annoyed you, then again I apologise,' he continued, casually trying to nudge Fern on to her feet.

'Yes, I am annoyed,' boomed the rabbit again, but then said in a quieter voice, 'but I accept your apology. However, you are not going one step further until you tell me what is going on.' He glared at Rowan, and then began to scratch again. Juniper was becoming more and more agitated, and kept looking longingly at the nearby trees, hoping to have an opportunity of darting up a nearby pine. The rabbit looked at him firmly, and Juniper decided that was not the proper course of action to take just at the moment.

Rowan decided that he had no option but to tell him the whole story. So quickly he recounted what had happened, starting with his friendship with Fern, and then how she had been captured and imprisoned by the grey squirrels, and how he and Juniper had just rescued her. He pointed to Fern's paws, and then the trail of blood, and the rabbit nodded.

'I tell you what I'll do,' he said. 'If you will remove this wretched bramble from my ear I'll help you.'

'But what can you do?' asked Rowan. 'I don't mean to be impolite, but we are in a terrible hurry and I can't see how you can help us.'

The rabbit looked at him in surprise, then hopped over to Fern and sniffed quickly around her.

'I could carry her on my back,' he said simply.

'Of course,' exclaimed Juniper.

Fern got up and stood before the rabbit. 'Put your head down,' she said. As he did so she began to part the matted hair around his enormous ears until, finally, she found the sharp thorn deeply embedded in the flesh. She pulled and prised but could not move it. She looked at it from all directions and sniffed it several times. Then with a cry of inspiration she bent forward and grasped the top of the thorn between her teeth. With a sharp pull, it was out.

'It's out. It's out,' cried Rowan. 'Now will you help us?'

The rabbit nodded, and squatted low on the ground. 'Climb up,' he said to Fern.

She tried vainly to get on to the rabbit's back, but his coat was so sleek she kept sliding off. Rowan and Juniper nudged and shoved her until, with a grunt from the rabbit, she was sitting astride him. She winced with pain, and the rabbit looked with despair at the mud, grime and blood that now stuck to his fur.

'Ouch!' he yelled. 'Don't pull my ears, or you can walk.'

'I'm sorry,' muttered Fern miserably. The pain in her feet was terrible, and she felt like crying. The rabbit seemed to sense this, and his voice became softer.

'Don't you worry, my little Thorn-Remover. I'll get you home safely.'

Juniper was getting agitated, his tail quivering madly.

'Whatever is the matter with you?' asked the rabbit, looking at Juniper with contempt.

Rowan smiled. 'I think he's anxious to get going.'

'Quite right. Quite right,' the rabbit replied. 'Hold tight, my dear. We're off.'

'By the way,' asked Rowan as they began to move, 'can you swim?'

'Can I swim? Can I swim? What sort of question is that?'

'Well,' replied Rowan, 'won't we have to cross the stream?'

'Oh, that. A mere puddle. Nothing to worry about. Not to a champion swimmer like me!'

A very strange sight indeed

Rowan could not help smiling at the rabbit's arrogance.

The creatures of the forest saw the strangest of sights that day, a rabbit carrying a grey squirrel on its back, and two red squirrels, all travelling together. Not long after they had passed, a hoard of angry grey squirrels rushed by, howling and yelling, and making terrible noises. Yes, a very strange sight indeed.

CHAPTER NINE

Rowan was amazed. His rescue party had just arrived back at Tolls Hill, and the meeting was still going on, still discussing what should be done and how the little grey squirrel could be saved. Proudly he and Juniper swaggered into the group, closely followed by the rabbit still carrying an injured and rather frightened Fern.

There was such excitement that all the red squirrels began talking at once.

'Where did you go?'

'How did you do it?'

'Were you frightened?'

'What did they do?'

'What did they say?'

Then they concentrated on Fern, who by now had slid painfully from the rabbit's back.

'Is this Fern?'

'Isn't she big?'

'Can she talk?'

Rowan and Juniper were overwhelmed with the noise, yet said nothing. Jasmine stepped forward and standing on her hind legs, called for silence.

'Be quiet, all of you. Can't you see she is hurt and frightened?'

Gradually calm settled on the group. Petal and Ivy moved close to Fern and spoke gently to her. After a while, several other females joined them, and between them they began to attend to Fern's injuries.

When the others had settled down Rowan and Juniper began to tell their tale, much to everyone's disbelief. There was complete silence as the story unfolded, but several horrified comments when they told of the jailors. A few squirrels had been surprised to hear that Fern had been kept in an old rabbit hole. Then there was a snort, and the rabbit decided it was time he was heard.

'I say,' he said curtly, 'there is nothing wrong with a rabbit living in a hole.'

'Oh, no,' declared Rowan, 'not for rabbits.'

The rabbit nodded. 'Quite so. Quite so.'

At that point Redfox interrupted. 'May I thank you for your help, Mr Rabbit.'

The rabbit let out a loud laugh. 'Mr Rabbit. I like it, I like it. Hah!'

'I'm sorry,' said Redfox, 'is that not your name?'

The rabbit grinned. 'My name is Nuthead,' he said proudly.

There was much sniggering and many of the squirrels began to giggle. The rabbit looked quite hurt. Rowan quickly said 'What a really.....unusual......name. Nuthead. It's very nice, Mr Nuthead.'

'Yes, I know,' replied the rabbit.

Suddenly there was a scuffle and a breathless, small squirrel sped through the group, looking frantically around him.

Moss stepped forward. 'What is the matter, Runner?'

'Grey squirrels,' he gasped. 'Lots of them. Heading this way.'

There were snorts and squeals of horror. Moss looked at Rowan and Juniper.

'What have you done?' he asked accusingly.

There was total confusion. Squirrels were squealing and tearing backwards and forwards in panic. Tails were jerking wildly and eyes were wide and frightened. Redfox tried to call everyone to order, but there was so much noise, he could not make himself heard. A wide-eyed squirrel started jumping up and down on the spot, teeth chattering and eyes rolling.

'We've had it. We've had it,' he screamed.

Chestnut cuffed him sharply across his ears and the squirrel, stunned, fell to the ground panting. Rowan just sat there watching. Thoughts of fighting rose in his mind. Then he remembered the size of the grey guards and dismissed the idea. There was nowhere to run to, the Grey Invaders would soon find them. What was to be done?

Suddenly there was a loud thumping, slow and methodical. One by one the squirrels stopped their squealing. It sounded like an earthquake.

'It's Nuthead,' cried Rowan, staring in surprise at the rabbit, 'Look at him.'

Sure enough, Nuthead was pounding the ground with one of his strong and powerful hind legs. The squirrels, now completely silent, watched the rabbit curiously. Then something strange happened. Gradually, first one at a time, then in twos and threes, rabbits from all over the hill emerged from their burrows. Nuthead continued to pound away and soon there were as many rabbits as squirrels.

By this time all the squirrels had gathered together. Nuthead glanced around, stopped his pounding, and stood up on his hind legs, towering above the squirrels.

'I have never witnessed such a scene in all my life,' he yelled, glaring at the animals around him. 'Where is your sense of self-preservation? Where is your courage? You can't just run around in circles and squeal every time you are in danger.'

He cast his eyes over the squirrels before him, and some were so ashamed they cowered before his gaze.

Nuthead turned to Redfox and the two animals had a short discussion. Redfox became excited and nodded his head again and again. The others watched quietly. Nuthead turned and ran over to the large gathering of waiting rabbits. Redfox moved to the centre of the quivering squirrels.

'There isn't much time,' he called, 'so listen carefully.'

Every single squirrel pricked its ears and became completely silent as they listened to what Redfox had to say. He told them of Nuthead's plan. He explained that they would form into groups of four, and that they would hide in the burrows with the rabbits. There were gasps and exclamations.

'The Grey Invaders will expect to find us in the tree-tops or hiding on the ground,' explained Redfox, 'but they will never dream of looking *under* the ground for us.'

'Brilliant!' yelled Rowan.

'Absolutely,' agreed Chestnut, and there were sounds of approval all around.

At that moment Nuthead returned. 'It's all arranged,' he said quickly, 'now let's get moving before it's too late.'

'Are you ready?' called Redfox, and there were shouts of 'Yes', and 'Let's go.'

'Get into groups of four and then go and join the rabbits,' Nuthead ordered.

There was an excited buzz as the squirrels began to argue about who was going with who. Redfox looked at Chestnut and sighed. They would all be too late.

The ground began to shake again. Rowan realised that Nuthead was pounding the earth fiercely.

'What on earth do you think you are doing?' shouted Nuthead. 'Get moving *now*!'

Jasmine was there with Fern, Ivy and Petal.

'Go, Mother,' urged Rowan, 'I will go with Juniper and Chestnut.' She nodded briefly and then all four scampered away.

Soon there were only a handful of squirrels left. All the others had disappeared with the rabbits. The hill was deserted - as if the squirrels had never been there. It was eerily quiet.

'The Grey Invaders will never find them,' whispered Nuthead. 'Come on, you four, come with me.'

They began to follow him. Rowan stopped suddenly. 'What's the matter, Rowan? We must hide now,' cried Chestnut. Rowan did not move.

'Look,' he said quickly, 'it's my fault that this has happened. I must go and check that everyone has hidden. There may still be some squirrels in a drey or out foraging.'

Chestnut swiftly moved to his brother's side and nudged him gently. 'That's very commendable, Rowan, but everyone would have heard the commotion, and they would certainly have heard Nuthead's pounding.'

Rowan glanced back at the trees in the wood thoughtfully. 'Come on, quickly!' called Nuthead. 'They'll be here shortly.'

'You're right, let's go,' replied Rowan. And with that they all disappeared down the nearest rabbit burrow.

The sun had hardly moved in the sky and barely a leaf had fallen from the trees when the first grey squirrels arrived. Scarface led them, teeth bared and nostrils flared. They rushed on to the hill, howling and bellowing and almost falling over each other in their eagerness for a fight.

Scarface paused then despatched his patrollers.

'You, and you. Up that tree there. Search all those dreys. You, check over there. You and you, those trees over there. *Now!'*

Every grey squirrel raced to obey as the orders were given. Scarface stood silently in the centre of the hill, listening and watching. One by one the patrollers returned, reporting that there were no red squirrels to be seen. Scarface growled and spat and cuffed the panting squirrels before him.

'Look again! They must be there.'

They raced away towards the empty dreys, terrified of the grey monster who yelled at them with teeth bared and eyes blazing, but there was not a sign of a red squirrel anywhere. As they returned, cowering and afraid, Scarface pawed the air and howled,

'I'll get them,' he screamed. 'Ill get them!'

They returned to Grey Squirrel Island, disillusioned and confused.

CHAPTER TEN

'It's started again,' declared the Owl.

The red and the grey squirrel nodded silently.

'They were very lucky,' the Owl continued, 'they may not be so fortunate next time.'

It was a hot and sultry day. The trip had been long and tiring and the Owl was none too pleased. He was anxious to get some sleep.

Amber was thinking about the unsettling news that they had just heard, when her attention was distracted by the laughing and squeals of delight coming from the youngsters playing on the ground below. She edged to the side of the drey and her whiskers flicked as she saw the red and grey squirrels playing happily together. She looked thoughtfully at Greybeard.

'If only it could be like this on Tolls Hill,' she murmured.

Greybeard nodded. 'We could go back and try and talk to them,' he said.

The Owl shook his head from side to side. 'No. Definitely not. The grey squirrels would kill you. Haven't you heard a word I've said?'

'If only I could talk to this squirrel called Fern,' whispered Amber. 'Maybe she would tell me whether some of the grey squirrels would leave the island and come and live here.'

Greybeard, who had been busily grooming his magnificent tail, looked up sharply. 'Now that's a good idea.'

The Owl sighed loudly and noisily.

'Don't you agree?' asked Amber politely.

'Of course I don't agree. What about Scarface, Thistle, Nettle and Ragwort and all the other males that follow Scarface? They would soon come and find this place, especially if they knew you two were here. Remember, I've been listening to them. They'll do anything. Go to any lengths. You must believe me.'

'But it's such a long way,' said Greybeard.

'Huh!' snorted the Owl, 'that would make little difference to them.'

Amber sighed again. 'I think he's right, Greybeard.'

'Of course I'm right,' snapped the Owl.

There was silence for a while, and the great bird began to close his eyes. He was so tired. No sleep all day, and it would soon be nightfall. Thank goodness those two squirrels had stopped asking questions. He liked them, of course. Why else would he have flown so far to tell them of the war that was brewing back on the hill? But now he was hungry, tired, and irritable. His eyelids fluttered and his head dropped slightly, sleep overcoming him.

'I've got it!' exclaimed Greybeard.

The Owl squawked and woke with a start. He glared at Greybeard who looked suitably apologetic.

'What, may I ask, have you got?' he hissed.

'The answer. I've got the answer.'

Amber was impressed by his excitement and listened eagerly.

'I was casting my mind back to when I used to live there. I forgot that Grey Squirrel Island is really an island.'

'Bravo,' said the Owl.

'No, please listen. I remember there was an awful storm one night and a huge tree was struck by fire from the sky. The tree exploded into hundreds of pieces. When we went out the next day we found the path of the river was blocked by the remains of the old tree and we could get across to Red Squirrel Island.'

'I don't understand,' whispered Amber.

But the Owl was awake now. 'I do,' he said, 'the broken tree must have dammed the river.'

'Exactly,' continued Greybeard, 'so if we could find the dam and destroy it........'

'The river would flow again,' declared the Owl.

'But I still don't quite understand.....' began Amber.

'Oh, for goodness' sake,' interrupted the Owl rudely, 'it's quite obvious, isn't it? If the river flows again the grey squirrels will be cut off on the island and won't be able to get across to Tolls Hill any more. Therefore, peace and harmony again!'

Amber looked apologetic. 'I'm still not quite clear.......surely the squirrels could swim across?'

Greybeard looked troubled. 'That's true, all squirrels can swim if they have to. So why couldn't they get across before the river was dammed?'

'I sometimes think my intelligence is wasted,' sighed the Owl. 'I would have thought it was quite obvious. When the fallen tree dammed the river the water was diverted and so the river flowed off in another direction. If the dam were destroyed, the water would come back with such force that even an otter would have difficulty in swimming through it. Certainly a squirrel would never be able to.'

Amber's whiskers twitched wildly and her tail flicked up and down excitedly. 'So if we could persuade any squirrels who wanted to leave to follow us, then the nasty squirrels like Scarface, Thistle, Nettle and Ragwort would be stranded there and would not be able to follow us?'

'Exactly!' said Greybeard.

There was great excitement in the drey that evening as they discussed their plans. The Owl promised to fly around the Island and look for the dam, then speak to Rowan and Fern. He would try and persuade them to go and meet Amber and Greybeard, somewhere far away from Grey Squirrel Island, so that they could be told of the plan.

It was growing dark, and the Owl stretched his magnificent wings.

'Now I am going home to eat, then I am going to sleep. It will be difficult to sleep in the dark, but I have no choice.'

Amber and Greybeard listened sympathetically to his moans and groans. They knew that he was the key to their success and they were trying very hard not to upset him.

The Owl and Greybeard were old friends, and, although the Owl found squirrels rather tiresome and silly creatures, he had no intention of letting them down. He rose from the drey and his powerful wings carried him swiftly away.

'Will it work?' asked Amber.

'It's got to,' Greybeard replied.

Before he left the next day the Owl, feeling very refreshed, was eagerly discussing the plan with the two squirrels. Greybeard, pausing in the conversation, flicked his ears affectionately at his friend.

'It's just like the old days,' he smiled. The Owl nodded.

'You helped us when we had to leave Tolls Hill, and now you are helping us again,' said Amber. 'We are very grateful to you.'

The Owl, preening, looked from one to the other. 'Greybeard saved my life, therefore I cannot do enough to repay him.'

Amber looked surprised, and turned to Greybeard questioningly. The grey squirrel nodded slowly.

'You can tell her,' said the Owl. Greybeard settled himself comfortably in the drey, and then began his tale:

'It was a long, long time ago. I was only a young squirrel but even then I had long fur on my chin, which is why I was called Greybeard. One day I was foraging in the woods on my own when suddenly I heard a terrible squawking. I was frightened, but curious to find out what was going on. I climbed up a nearby tree and looked all around. Then I saw a huge fox. It had an enormous bushy tail, piercing eyes and large white teeth as sharp as a holly leaf. I could see his teeth clearly because in his mouth he held a bird. The poor thing was crying for help, but there were no other animals around. They had all run away because of the fox.'
Amber had noticed that the Owl had begun to quiver. She nudged him gently. 'The bird was you, wasn't it?' she whispered. He did not reply but she knew.

'Yes,' Greybeard continued, 'the bird was the Owl. He was not very old and had fallen out of his nest whilst his mother was away hunting. Unfortunately the fox found him before he had a chance to find help. Anyway, I had never seen a fox before and did not really know how dangerous it was. The Owl kept crying out, so I ran down the tree and told the fox off.'

'Good gracious!' exclaimed Amber.

Greybeard smiled. 'You must remember I was very young, and did not know what I was doing. The fox obviously thought I was crazy and tried to ignore me. But the Owl kept on calling to me to help and I couldn't just leave him. When the fox tried to pass me I stood in his way. The fox was appalled at my stupidity. He turned quickly and with a flick of his tail, he sent me flying.'

He paused briefly, noticing that Amber and the Owl were completely silent, listening to his every word. 'For a moment I lay there, wondering what to do. Then the fox turned again and walked over me as if I wasn't there. So I bit his foot.'

Amber gasped.

'Yes,' he said proudly, 'I bit his foot. Hard. He yelled, and as he yelled he dropped Owl. Everything happened very quickly. At that precise moment the Owl's mother, who had been watching helplessly in a tree, dived on the fox. He was so taken by surprise that he crouched down low on the ground. I jumped on to his other foot and bit that too. You should have heard him howl! Then Owl's mother landed on the fox's back and sunk her claws deep into his flesh. Blood poured out. He was such a coward, he howled even louder. Finally he raced off into the woods and Owl's mother and I quickly went over to the youngster to see if he was alright.'

'Thankfully, I was,' said the Owl softly, 'all thanks to you.'

'How wonderful,' sighed Amber.

'And so you see,' continued the Owl, 'I will do everything that I can to help you. Now I must set off for Tolls Hill. I will try and speak to Fern and Rowan, and Jasmine and Redfox too.'

Greybeard and Amber stood up as their friend prepared to depart. 'Don't forget that we will meet them on Hungry Hill the day after tomorrow.'

'Don't worry, I won't,' called the Owl as he took to the air.

Greybeard moved over to Amber's side. 'Jasmine will understand. As soon as Owl tells her about us, she will talk to Fern.'

Amber nodded. 'She will be so surprised when Owl tells her we are still alive.'

CHAPTER ELEVEN

Jasmine froze as a dark shadow fell on the ground in front of her. Forcing herself to look up she saw the great bird flying over her. Its wings were huge, much bigger than those of the hawk.

'It's a monster,' she thought as she began to run. She heard the bird calling to her, but refused to listen. It was a giant hawk trying to fool her. She must not listen. She thought she heard him call her name. They were clever, these monsters.

She dashed into the undergrowth, knowing the bird would not be able to follow her because of the dense trees. She cowered low.

'Tut, tut. For goodness' sake,' said the bird.

Jasmine looked up in alarm to see the bird perched on the tree above her.

She shook her head, determined not to listen. She knew she was safe for the moment. He could not reach her.

'Are you Jasmine?' asked the bird.

No reply.

'For goodness' sake. Will you answer me? Are you Jasmine?'

Still no reply. She heard the bird give a deep sigh.

'You silly squirrel. Will you listen to me? Amber sent me.'

'I don't believe you,' said Jasmine, looking at the bird carefully.

'My dear squirrel,' said the Owl impatiently, 'I really don't care whether you believe me or not. I just want to talk to Rowan and Fern.'

Jasmine looked at the great bird in bewilderment. How did he know Amber?

'If you really know Amber, then tell me where she is,' demanded Jasmine.

She listened quietly as the bird told her about Amber and Greybeard, living in some far off place with other red and grey squirrels.

'Please tell me more about the place where they live,' she said. The Owl sighed and began to describe it as best as he could.

She shook her head, determined not to listen.

It was then that Rowan came across his mother and the great bird, deep in conversation. He immediately thought of the incident with the hawk, and was horrified. The bird had got his mother talking, and intended to kill her and eat her, he was sure. Without a thought for his own safety, he rushed over to Jasmine and, placing himself between her and the bird, began to scream.

'Quickly, Mother. Go. Don't listen to what he is saying. Run, mother. *Run*!'

The Owl peered at Rowan with contempt. 'This, I assume, is Rowan?'

Jasmine's whiskers twitched with amusement. Rowan, facing the Owl and with his back to his mother, could not see the grin on her face.

'Oh, no. He knows my name.'

The bird looked from Jasmine to Rowan, and back to Jasmine again.

'Do I have to endure this?' he asked with a sigh.

Jasmine gently nudged her son. Rowan, thinking that his mother had gone, jumped into the air with fright.

'It's alright, Rowan,' she said softly. 'He's a friend.'

'A friend?' he replied hoarsely, 'but it's a hawk.'

'Hmph!' exclaimed the bird, 'I am an Owl. A very wise Owl, I might add. I am certainly not a hawk.' He pouted and puffed for some time. 'What an insult,' he moaned.

Jasmine was explaining to Rowan all that the Owl had told her. 'I think we must listen to what he has to say,' she said. Rowan nodded in agreement and apologised to the Owl.

'You must think I am very silly,' he said.

'Not that silly. Just a typical red squirrel. Thank goodness for Greybeard, that's all I can say.'

At that, Jasmine made a decision. 'I think you had better go and get Fern,' she told Rowan, 'and I will go and find Redfox. I think he should be in on this.'

As the two squirrels scampered away, the Owl sighed loudly. He was hot and tired and hungry again. He glanced up at the brilliant sunshine and sneezed. He hated being hot. He ought to be in the middle of a nice dark wood, high up in a tree, fast asleep. The sooner I get these squirrels sorted out, he thought, the sooner my life will be back to normal.

Fern stood quivering beside a bunch of dandelions, her eyes flickering and her nostrils flaring.

'Please, Fern, do hurry. Mother will be angry,' implored Rowan.

Still she refused to go any further.

'Mother says it's not a hawk, Fern. It's a friend.'

Fern's glazed eyes showed no response. Rowan was getting angry and frustrated. He did not know just how long he had been sitting beside Fern, trying to get her to join Jasmine and Redfox and the Owl. He had nudged her, encouraged her, sympathised with her, and bullied her, all to no avail. Finally he left her and scurried over to the waiting group.

'She won't come,' he said, eyeing the Owl warily.

'She must,' declared the Owl.

Redfox and Jasmine were talking earnestly. Jasmine paused, and looked over to Fern.

'She's afraid of him,' said Rowan looking at the bird. There was a loud hiss and all three squirrels jumped in fright. The Owl hissed again.

'She must come, that's all there is to it. I've told you briefly the plan. Amber needs to talk to Fern and so she has got to come.'

Rowan looked from the Owl to his mother and Redfox. 'What plan?'

Jasmine began moving over towards Fern. 'You explain to him, Redfox, while I go and talk to her,' she called.

Redfox began explaining to Rowan. The Owl closed his eyes and tried to rest. This was the third time they had been over 'The Plan' and he knew it upside down, inside out, backwards, forwards and sideways. They were deep in conversation. So the Owl dozed.

A short while later Jasmine and Fern arrived. Fern made sure that at least one squirrel was between her and the great bird. The other two squirrels stopped talking and Redfox turned to Jasmine.

'Have you explained it all to her?'

'Yes,' she replied, 'she will go with Rowan, but she doesn't know whether she will be any help or not.'

'Well, Amber certainly thinks so. I don't know what you think, Jasmine, but I feel that these two youngsters are hardly able to travel to Hungry Hill on their own.'

'I agree, Redfox,' she replied. 'Should we ask Chestnut and Juniper to go with them?'

'That's a good idea,' said Redfox thoughtfully. 'In the meantime I will take Moss and Runner and see if we can find the dam with the information Owl has given us.'

There was a shuffle behind them, and a loud cough.

'May I be permitted to assist?'

'Nuthead!' exclaimed Rowan and Fern. They scampered over to greet their friend. Nuthead wandered over to the group and sat on his haunches and began cleaning his whiskers. Rowan and Fern sat beside their friend, Fern sniffing at the rabbit's ear to see how the thorn wound was healing. The Owl, who everyone thought was asleep, opened his eyes and glared at the rabbit.

'How do you think you can help?' said the Owl almost sneeringly.

'It's simple,' cried Rowan, 'he knows how to get to Grey Squirrel Island. He can take you there, Redfox.'

The rabbit nodded and the Owl scowled. Redfox agreed. 'Brilliant. Thank you Nuthead. And thank you Mr Owl.' He turned to Jasmine. 'Quickly then, go and get Juniper and Chestnut. There is no time to lose. The Owl will show them the way.'

He turned and hurried into the wood, pausing momentarily to call to Rowan and Fern. 'Good luck, all of you. Good luck.'

CHAPTER TWELVE

It was a dull and misty day on Grey Squirrel Island. Scarface was in a bad mood and had called for everyone to come and sit before him. He was furious that the guards had lost their prisoner and demanded that they come before him. Reluctantly the two crept forward. Scarface hissed and spat at them and, raising his gleaming claws, slashed at their faces and backs. They howled in pain.

'Incompetent fools!' he screamed.

The mass of watching squirrels said nothing but there was an unmistakable look of horror on their faces. In a frenzy Scarface jumped on the two and tore at their flesh with his teeth. Then he called to Thistle.

'Take them away.....and kill them!'

Still no one spoke. They looked at each other, terrified. Thistle edged forward.

'Now!' boomed Scarface. Thistle jumped and beckoning to two patrollers, dragged the two guards away. Scarface then turned to the others.

'They are no better than the red squirrels. Traitors. Useless fools. They are no good to me. I need squirrels I can rely on. Can I rely on you?' He glared at the faces around him.

Still no one answered.

'Well?' he yelled loudly. 'Can I?' His eyes were piercing. The squirrels were afraid. Slowly they began to mumble.

'Yes. Yes.' Then a few patrollers, feeling more confident, moved amongst the group, biting those that did not respond and chanting themselves; eventually most of the group were shouting:

'Yes. You can rely on us, Scarface.'

Scarface calmed down and the glazed look left his eyes.

'I need to know I can rely on you all,' he said, his voice softening. 'You see, grey squirrels are fighters. If you are too frightened to fight then there is no place for you on Grey Squirrel Island. How do you think we have got this island to ourselves? Because of our strength and power. No one dares challenge us.

Even the stoats think twice about attacking us. We are all-powerful and the rulers of the island. Red squirrels are like infants, frightened and docile and pathetic. We need to let them know that we are in control.'

'But the red squirrels have gone from Tolls Hill,' called Nettle. Scarface glared at him for daring to interrupt his speech.

'They appear to have left, yes, that is true. They must have gone somewhere. We will enlist the help of the birds, the rabbits, the rats and the mice until we find out exactly where they have gone.'

'But the other animals won't talk, they are all afraid of us,' declared Nettle, unperturbed by Scarface's scowls.

'That's right,' murmured some of the others.

'Shut up,' shouted Scarface, his voice rising louder and louder, 'don't argue with me, I know what I'm talking about. We will force them to co-operate. Threaten to kill their infants if they do not help us. Tell the birds we will break up their nests and destroy their eggs. Let the rabbits know that we will tell the fox where their burrows are.'

'The rats will help,' called a patroller.

'Brilliant. Go and talk to the rats.'

There were murmurings amongst the group, but Scarface ignored them. 'Go now, all of you, and get to work. I want to find out where those red squirrels have gone. I won't rest until we have captured every last one of them.'

The squirrels scampered away quickly, shaking their heads and looking over their shoulders at their leader. He was so mean, spiteful and awesome. They dare not disobey.

The only squirrel that stayed on was Nettle, and he and Scarface eyed each other for a long moment before Nettle finally spoke.

'You've gone too far.'

'Oh, be quiet. You're as bad as the reds. Call yourself a grey squirrel? You're pathetic.'

Nettle began to sharpen his claws against a nearby tree bark.

'You don't scare me, you know. I'll take you on any day.'

'Is that so?' cried Scarface, and jumped high into the air, landing behind Nettle. He stood up on his hind legs whilst Nettle was still turning to face him and with a mighty swing tried to tear open Nettle's back, but Nettle jumped away from Scarface, narrowly avoiding the attack. He turned in mid-air and managed to twist his body so he would land facing his attacker. They both bared their teeth and snorted, then Nettle leapt at Scarface.

Clinging together they rolled and tumbled, biting and kicking as they did so. Clumps of fur flew through the air. Grabbing a sturdy twig in his mouth Scarface swept it across his opponent's back, causing Nettle to cry out in pain. Scarface laughed and gave a long, haunting howl. Nettle pounced, sinking his teeth into the leader's neck. With a spin and a kick Scarface broke free.

On and on they fought, oblivious to what was going on around. One by one, the squirrels returned, attracted by the sounds of the fighting and the yells of rage. Frightened by the scene before them, they cringed behind trees and foliage and peered from the tree-tops.

As the mighty squirrels lay panting side by side after a punishing bout, Thistle suddenly appeared at the side of Scarface.

'Get him,' hissed Scarface, and Thistle, hesitating only briefly, launched himself on Nettle, biting and tearing at his ears and his cheeks and gouging large gashes in his side. Eventually, exhausted and mortally wounded, Nettle hobbled away. Behind him, Scarface proudly held Nettle's tail in his paws. Everyone knew, the ultimate humiliation for a squirrel was to lose his tail. Poor Nettle.

All the watching squirrels quickly hurried away, leaving Thistle and Scarface triumphantly licking their wounds.

CHAPTER THIRTEEN

'I can't see him.'

'I can. Look, over there by those brambles.'

'That's not him. It's a piece of wood.'

'It's not. It's got ears.'

'It's a log, I tell you.'

'I bet it isn't.'

'Is that him over there?'

'Where?'

'Up there. Look. Flying over those trees.'

'No, silly. That's a seagull.'

'I bet it's him.'

'It is not, I tell you.'

'Well, where is he, then?'

'I don't know.'

The four squirrels stood together. They had lost the Owl and had no idea where they were. They had been travelling for such a long time, their legs ached and they were all quite tired. There were several acorns laying around, but they were all too nervous to eat. Fern began whimpering. The familiar sound of Juniper's chattering teeth began.

'What shall we do, Chestnut?' asked Rowan miserably.

'I'm thinking,' was the reply.

'Could you think a little quicker?' asked Rowan. Chestnut glared at his brother. He could not understand it. One minute that Owl was there, and the next he had disappeared. If the bird had deserted them, they were doomed. He had no idea of the way back to Tolls Hill; the Owl had been keeping a keen eye open for foxes and stoats.

Suddenly there was the sound of rushing wind and the Owl landed on a nearby bramble bush. 'Sorry for the delay. Supper.'

'Supper?' shouted Chestnut, trying to control his emotions. He was so pleased to see the bird, and yet angry that he had left them alone.

'That's right,' replied the Owl. 'Supper. And if you are wise you will eat all you can here. We will soon reach Hungry Hill.'

'Why is it called Hungry Hill?' asked Juniper, struggling to control his grinding teeth. The Owl stretched himself stiffly. 'Because it's just open fields. No woods, no bushes, no copses, nothing. Just fields.'

'But why *Hungry* Hill?' persisted Juniper.

'Because there is no food, of course,' the Owl retorted.

'Oh, of course.'

The Owl, feeling slightly refreshed after his meal, let it pass. 'Are you ready to continue?'

Fern looked imploringly at Rowan. 'It's getting dark. I'm frightened, Rowan.'

Rowan nodded and turned to Chestnut. He had heard her. 'It is getting a bit dim,' he explained to the Owl, 'shouldn't we find somewhere to rest for the night and take some food?'

The Owl thought for a moment. It was true night was coming; the moon was already rising. Night was a dangerous time for squirrels, he knew that. Foxes lurked in the shadows, stoats patrolled, even a few of his fellow Owls might look upon the little squirrels as a good meal.

'There's a barn coming up,' he said. 'You can rest there and I will fly ahead and tell Amber and Greybeard what is happening.'

Fern sighed with relief and secretly Juniper, Chestnut and Rowan were relieved too. They were all exhausted and very hungry. Rowan grabbed a few leaves as they followed the Owl. Juniper rooted amongst the hedgerows for berries. Chestnut collected a few acorns and Fern carried a dandelion stem.

The barn towered above them. It was dark, mysterious and frightening. They peered inside cautiously. Strange shadows moved silently. An old wooden door creaked backwards and forwards in the wind. The smell of the place was frightening too. Damp, musty. It was all so unfamiliar. They had never been inside a building before, and begged the Owl to let them climb a tree. The Owl shook his head quickly.

'No good. There are no dreys here. If it rains you'll get sick and I can't risk that. Just go inside that opening there and snuggle into the hay. It will be quite safe. I'll be back soon to keep watch.'

They pushed and shoved Fern into the massive structure and almost buried themselves in the soft, warm hay. Rowan wrinkled his nose and sniffed, sneezing and snorting.

'It smells nice,' he laughed. Juniper nibbled a few wisps and declared it to be very good.

'We'll be alright here,' smiled Chestnut, 'but please hurry back to keep watch.'

'Will do,' called the Owl as he moved away, 'but keep an eye open until I get back. Any strange noises, hide in the hay.'

They watched as the Owl flew off, then bounced on the pile of hay, happily chewing berries and sucking in the thin strands of sweet dried grasses. Fern had to be encouraged to eat, but soon all were full and relaxed. It was not long before they were all fast asleep. No one remembered to keep watch.

In the corner of the barn sat two black rats. They had been silently watching the antics of the young squirrels for some time. They whispered hoarsely to each other, nodded, and then one of them crept towards the sleeping Fern who was laying near the edge of the hay.

Closer and closer he crept. Silently, like a shadow. He noted her breathing. Regular, shallow. She was fast asleep. An easy prey.

He could smell her fur now. She would make a tasty meal. He began to drool. He was so close he could feel the warmth of her body. He positioned himself ready to pounce.

Suddenly there was a screech. All the squirrels woke up at the same time, startled by the noise. They watched in amazement as the Owl swooped by Fern and grabbed something long and black.

'It looks like a rat!' whispered Chestnut. Fern began to cry as the Owl carried his prisoner away and out into the night. They heard the rat howling.

Back in the corner the other rat, who had been watching, crept furtively away.

When the Owl returned he told the squirrels he was disgusted to see them fast asleep with no one on watch. They looked so sorrowful and frightened that he decided not to be too hard on them.

'What...what happened to it?' asked Juniper.

The Owl stretched his wings, adjusted a few feathers, and shrugged. 'Let's just say he won't be back,' he said.

The squirrels huddled together, murmuring to each other. The Owl felt sorry for them.

'Look. I'm here now. I'll be on guard. You try and get some sleep,' he said.

He flew up to the top of the barn and positioned himself on one of the rafters of the building where he could keep a careful watch on his travelling companions. From the corner of his eye he noticed a movement and turning his head saw a young barn owl just a little way away from him. They nodded courteously to each other. Hesitatingly, the youngster moved closer until they were almost touching.

'What's going on?' he asked softly.

'Keeping an eye on them,' said the Owl, nodding towards the sleeping group. He then began to tell the story of his companion. Owls are friendly birds and enjoy each other's company. Quite some time passed as the Owl told of the saga of the grey and red squirrels. The youngster sat quietly whilst the story was told. When the Owl had finished, he hooted softly.

'There may be a problem,' he said, and told the Owl of the other rat and his suspicious behaviour. The Owl nodded, asked the youngster to continue keeping watch, and disappeared.

The next morning, as the party of squirrels set out feeling refreshed and excited, no one noticed the two dead rats laying in the undergrowth.

The landscape began to change. The trees began to thin out, and the hedges got lower and lower. Eventually there was nothing to be seen but never-ending fields, stretching away as far as the eye could see.

Abruptly, Chestnut, who was leading, stopped and turned round.

'Look behind you,' he gasped. They all stopped and turned. They had been climbing steadily, and had almost reached the top of a very steep hill. There was almost nothing to be seen but sky.

'This must be Hungry Hill,' said Chestnut.

'That's correct,' said a female voice. It seemed to come from beyond the crest of the hill they were climbing. They stood in amazement as a female red squirrel and a male grey squirrel appeared ahead of them.

The female was magnificent. Her tail was brilliant red like an autumn sunset. It glistened as she moved. She had impressive tufts on her ears, and her eyes sparkled. The grey was quite the biggest squirrel they had ever seen. Even Rowan, who had seen Scarface and Thistle, was astounded.

Fern's immediate reaction was to run to the grey squirrel and sniff him excitedly. They touched noses. Then Rowan, Juniper and Chestnut did the same with the red squirrel.

'We have much to discuss, little squirrels,' said Greybeard, 'and little time to do so. Fern, will you go and talk to Amber?'

After a slight pause, Fern approached the red female, and they sniffed each other.

'You're a good squirrel, Fern,' whispered Amber, 'and we need your help so badly.'

The others squatted together quietly whilst the females spoke at length. Greybeard whispered to the Owl.

'Will you watch for us, old friend?'

The bird nodded and rose into the sky above them. There was nothing to be heard but the rush of wind as the Owl left, and the hushed whisperings of the two female squirrels.

A gentle mist began to descend, which gave them further protection whilst they formulated their plan. Amber and Fern, who had eventually joined the others, had obviously become firm friends. Fern's timidity was gone and she found herself joining in the excited chatter as the finer points were discussed.

Finally, every detail had been covered, and Greybeard spoke with gentle authority.

'We dare not return with you, for if the grey squirrels heard of our presence, they would attack again.'

Chestnut nodded. 'We understand,' he murmured.

'You know what has to be done. I hope that it will not be too long before we shall all be together, and living without fear of the Grey Invaders. Good luck to you all.'

Rowan felt an involuntary shudder travel from the back of his neck to the tip of his tail. He touched noses with Amber and Greybeard, as did the others, then they began the long trek home. The Owl was there, showing the way through the mist.

Amber and Greybeard stood and watched them go, until the mist enveloped them. Then they turned wistfully to each other.

'Do you think it will work?'

'It must. It must.'

Amber sighed. 'How lovely if we could return to Tolls Hill one day'

Greybeard nudged his mate affectionately. 'Who knows?' he replied.

CHAPTER FOURTEEN

Rowan stretched carefully in the drey. Fern lay beside him, together with Jasmine, Juniper and Chestnut. So much had happened recently, his mind felt as if it was spinning. His legs still ached from the long trek to Hungry Hill and back. His throat hurt and he wondered why. Then he thought of all the talking he had done since his return.

At long last, however, a decision had been made and 'The Plan' was going to be put into action the following day. He was very excited about that, but he was still so tired. If only he could sleep for a little while. He stretched again and suddenly his mother was nuzzling his ear.

'Try and get some sleep, Rowan.'

He wriggled closer to her. 'Mother?' he whispered, anxious not to wake the others.

'What is it?'

'Where are Petal and Ivy?'

Jasmine smiled and her eyes glistened as she replied, 'I told you earlier, Rowan. They have found mates and now have dreys of their own.'

Rowan was puzzled. 'But why would they want to leave our drey?'

Jasmine paused for a moment, and then took a deep breath and attempted to explain to her inquisitive son. 'Ivy and Petal are older than you. When squirrels reach a certain age they must find mates of their own, and so have their own dreys where they can raise their families.'

'Oh,' said Rowan thoughtfully, 'you mean like Amber and Greybeard?'

'Yes, exactly,' said Jasmine with relief.

'Or.....'

'Or what, Rowan?'

'Or maybe like Fern and I?'

Jasmine gasped and tried to make it sound like a cough.

Goodness, was this really Rowan, her youngest son?

'Go to sleep, Rowan.'

'But, Mother....'

'Go to sleep.'

Jasmine nipped him playfully on his ear, and then settled herself down in the comfortable drey. How quickly time passed by, she thought.

The squirrels on Tolls Hill were up and about before the sun rose the next day. Every single one had been given a task to do and each carried out their instructions without question. They knew that the survival of them all depended on their efforts.

Even though they were so busy each one of them still marvelled at the beautiful colours around them as the sun began to rise. The sky turned from grey to yellow, red and blue. The edges of the trees glistened from the morning dew as the rays of the sun caught them. The squirrels began to feel the warmth of the sunshine on their faces and as the ground began to warm too a soft grey mist began to rise.

'This is what we are fighting for,' thought Rowan, looking around him in wonder, 'to be able to continue to live here without fear. To be able to wake each morning and enjoy the colours and sights that the sun brings in the morning.'

Taking a deep breath of the fresh, crisp air he hurried away.

Three groups of squirrels now stood quietly and expectantly at the bottom of the hill, just outside Rowan's wood. One group were the larger adult males, who were busily preening and gnawing their teeth in anticipation. This group were fighters, the ones who would go to Grey Squirrel Island and bring back as many grey squirrels as were willing to come. Those that were not prepared to leave the Island, such as the guards and patrollers and those that followed Scarface, would have to be dealt with if 'The Plan' were to stand any hope of succeeding. This group was under the leadership of Redfox. Amongst them were Juniper and Chestnut.

The second group consisted of younger males. They, too, were busily grooming their coats and tails. They were nervous, but quiet, as they had been instructed. In charge of this group was Runner, who with the help of Moss and Rowan was to lead them to the dam. They all knew their objective - to bite and claw their way through the trees and branches that dammed the river, so that the water would be released, and once again separate Grey Squirrel Island from Tolls Hill.

The last group were the females and infants, all fearful for their sons and fathers. Their job was to meet the grey squirrels that the first group brought back and welcome them, then take them to the dreys as quickly as possible. Amongst them were Ivy, Petal and Jasmine. Only Jasmine knew the contingency plan - if there was trouble and the river did not flow, or Scarface and the others got out, then they had to save the infants. They had to run, as fast as they could, towards Hungry Hill. She shuddered.

At the front of the three groups stood Nuthead and the Owl, murmuring together. The Owl had been given the task of reporting progress, flying high between all three groups. Nuthead's job was to carry any injured back to Tolls Hill. He was not looking forward to his task. He would rather be up front, fighting. But the squirrels had insisted.

There was a rustle in the trees before them, and Moss appeared, gasping for breath.

'She's there,' he panted. 'She's on the island.'

A murmur went round the waiting squirrels. Rowan looked at Jasmine, who winked at him and wrinkled her nose affectionately. He was so proud of Fern for agreeing to return to Grey Squirrel Island to talk to the other grey squirrels. But what a risk she took. If she was recognised by the guards, or if one of the squirrels reported her, she would be killed. Of that he had no doubt.

Moss was speaking to Redfox.

'We have to give her time, but there's no telling how long it will take to free the water.'

Redfox nodded thoughtfully. 'Group Two,' he called to the waiting squirrels, 'it's time to go. Do the best that you can, and good luck.'

Quickly and quietly they ran off, following Runner and Rowan. They entered the wood and Rowan immediately felt at ease as he followed the familiar path. Some of the others whimpered involuntarily, but not one of them considered turning back. Tolls Hill was their home, and it was worth fighting for, even if it were to the bitter end.

As Rowan expected, the trees grew thicker and the wood darker. He whispered to Runner.

'I think it would be a good idea to go through the tree-tops. It will put the others at their ease.'

Runner readily agreed. The group thankfully hurried up the nearest tree away from the menacing dark below.

Back on the hill, Group One was waiting. Redfox was speaking to the Owl and Nuthead, but not one other squirrel spoke. Then Redfox turned to his group.

'It is time. You know what has to be done. Are you ready?'

'Yes,' came the reply.

Redfox turned to Jasmine. 'Good luck,' he whispered.

'And to you,' she replied.

He turned then, and was about to head off into the wood when the Owl let out a loud hoot. Redfox jumped around.

'Look,' squealed the Owl. 'Look over there.'

All eyes turned to where the Owl was facing, curious to see what had aroused such a reaction in the rather moody bird. Coming down the hill were two large squirrels, one grey, and one red. Behind them scurried about twenty younger squirrels, some red, some grey.

'Amber,' gasped Jasmine, and ran to the red squirrel and touched noses. Now there was much excitement on the hill. All of the squirrels had heard the story of Amber and Greybeard, and now these legendary animals stood before them.

Greybeard addressed himself to Redfox. 'We felt we could not let you go through this on your own. We have come to help.'

Amber moved over to Greybeard's side. 'I may not be able to do much,' she said, 'but Greybeard will help you fight, if necessary.'

Even Redfox was awestruck by the size of Greybeard. He stood high on his tiptoes and stretched his neck until it ached. Still he barely reached Greybeard's chin. Redfox gave up and crouched low against the ground, unsure how he should react. The grey squirrel, aware that he towered somewhat over the red squirrel, crouched likewise before Redfox. This immediately put Redfox at his ease, and the two touched noses.

'We will need you,' said Redfox softly.

'I know,' was the hushed reply. The two looked at each other for a moment, and then Redfox called to his group.

'Time to go.'

He turned towards the wood. He and Greybeard led the others through the outer trees and into the heart of the forest. The females, watching them go, waved goodbye. Each one of them was afraid but they knew that they had a job to do too. Amber came and sat beside Jasmine.

'Are you thinking about what happened before?'

Jasmine nodded silently. She closed her eyes as the memories of the earlier battle of the Grey Invaders came flooding back. Pictures again of the forest floor crimson with the blood of squirrels, of family and friends dead and dying, of the broken and crumpled body of Jasmine's mate. Tears rolled down her face.

'What happened to you?' whispered Jasmine. Amber moaned. 'It was a terrible time, as you know. Greybeard was devastated. He felt it was our fault that the massacre had happened, because someone had found out about us. I had to drag him away, although he wanted to give his life.' Amber looked around her wistfully. 'He loved Tolls Hill, you know, and every red squirrel here. Never once did I hear him complain about leaving Grey Squirrel Island or being the only grey on the hill. He wanted to go and hunt down Scarface and kill him. I convinced him that doing so would only bring the greys back again. If Scarface believed him dead, then perhaps they would not come back. So we left the hill hoping that the greys would think we had been killed too.'

Jasmine stroked her friend's face as tears began to fall down her cheeks. 'We ran and ran, it seemed for so long. I was blinded by tears and Greybeard refused to talk to me because he felt he should have stayed on and slain Scarface. We had no idea where we were going; we just kept going on and on. We began to worry because there were fewer and fewer trees. We thought a hawk might see us, or a fox. There was no shelter. Then we found an old rabbit burrow and crept in there for the first two days. Greybeard would creep out at dusk and dawn to find some food. I just stayed in the burrow. Then on the third day Greybeard persuaded me to come out and we started running again.'

'It must have been awful,' said Jasmine, 'not having a drey to go to.'

Amber nodded. 'It was. Anyway, by that time Owl had caught up with us, having heard what had happened. He flew ahead to see where we could go; eventually he returned and told us he had found a copse with lots of pine trees, oaks, chestnuts, and a stream and that there were no other squirrels there. First we came to Hungry Hill...'

'Where you met the others recently?'

'That's right. Hungry Hill is a terrible place with barely any food or shelter. Owl insisted we kept going and eventually we came to Sleeping Wood. It was such a quiet and tranquil place and after the last few days we had had it seemed ideal. Not nearly so nice as Tolls Hill, but the best we could find. The Owl said that there was little else ahead.'

Amber sighed deeply. 'So we built our drey and called it home. Greybeard grew more cheerful as time went on. I think perhaps he had begun to forget.'

Jasmine nodded and nudged her friend gently. 'And were you happy?'

'Yes, I was happy. I was with Greybeard, after all. Several seasons passed. It was so different from what had been...... I knew Greybeard would one day want to return to Tolls Hill, that he had to repay his debt to the red squirrels. And now it seems that time has come.'

Jasmine and Amber lay close together, their bodies quivering with fear and anticipation. If 'The Plan' worked, then the future would be really exciting for all of them. They would be able to live together, red and grey squirrels, without fear.

CHAPTER FIFTEEN

Fern was sitting at the top of a pine tree, watching a group of female greys foraging below. She knew most of them; they had grown up together. She looked carefully all around. There was no sign of any guards. Taking a deep breath she tried to think how best to tell them. She knew what she had to do. She had to explain about Amber and Greybeard, she had to tell them about Tolls Hill and she had to convince them that red and grey squirrels could live together as friends. Would they believe her?

She watched as they shared pine cones together, and smiled when one of the young females carried over some fungi. She recalled the last time she had eaten the succulent food, with Rowan at their 'special place'. She sighed. It seemed so long ago now.

'Hello, Fern.'

She jumped and turned quickly.

'My, you are jumpy.'

She swivelled round quickly but could see no other squirrel. She felt her hackles rising along her back.

'Who are you?' she whispered. There was a rustle on the tree beside her, and a grey squirrel appeared, beaming.

'Sunbeam!'

The two animals touched noses, and Fern, so delighted to see one of her old friends again, nuzzled the newcomer repeatedly.

'Steady on,' laughed Sunbeam. 'You'll have me off this tree.'

They giggled together. 'I'm so pleased to see you, Fern. They told me you had been sent away.'

Fern looked sad. 'It's a long story, Sunbeam.'

'Then let's hear it,' he said.

Fern turned and looked at the group below and Sunbeam followed her gaze.

'Can we join the others, then I can tell all of you about it.'

Fern hesitated. She had to trust her friends and she was anxious because time was getting short. She followed Sunbeam down the tree and was greeted with excitement. Immediately she regained her confidence and began to tell her story.

From above, the Owl watched the scene and listened to what was being said. Things seemed to be going well there. He flew quickly in a circle, unseen by the squirrels below, and headed off to see how the others were doing.

He was flying swiftly over the tree-tops when he thought he saw some movement below. Quickly he dived lower and there saw Nuthead, carrying a small red squirrel on his back. The Owl dropped to the ground in front of the rabbit.

'Surely the fighting hasn't started already?' he asked Nuthead.

'No, it hasn't,' replied the rabbit sharply.

'What happened?' he persisted.

Nuthead sat down and the young squirrel slid from his back and landed on the ground with a gentle thud.

'This is one of the youngsters from group three. He thought he could help with the fighting.' Nuthead winked at the Owl. 'Redfox thought he would be better looking after the females, so I am taking him back.'

Up till now, the Owl and the rabbit had not got on very well, tolerating each other and only conversing when absolutely necessary. Now they knew they both had to work together. The success of 'The Plan' could depend on it.

The Owl leant forward and whispered to Nuthead.

'Tell you what. There's not much happening at the moment. Why don't I take him back for you?'

Nuthead looked curiously at the bird, and then smiled knowingly. 'Capital idea.'

The great bird then lifted gently into the air, hovering above the cowering squirrel. He grasped him firmly by the scruff of the neck and rose swiftly into the air and flew away towards the hill.

'Mmmm,' thought Nuthead. 'Not a bad sort. Not bad at all.'

The squirrels in Redfox's group lay alert in the undergrowth. No one made a sound; even when the occasional screech or scream of a squirrel came from the island they kept quiet. Redfox had to admit that he was amazed. He looked around him with interest. There was plenty of food, pine cones and chestnut leaves. He was about to take a bite when there was a flapping above him. Owl had arrived.

'I can see the first group of grey squirrels coming,' the bird reported, and then soared quickly away. Redfox turned and there was Fern running along the ground, closely followed by about a dozen nervous females. Fern and Redfox touched noses briefly.

'Well done, Fern. Well done.'

He moved swiftly to the squirrels behind her. 'Welcome. Welcome. Please follow us.'

The grey squirrels were not sure what to do, but they saw that Fern had no fear and so, after only a brief hesitation, followed the red squirrels away from Grey Squirrel Island.

Fern watched them go for a moment, then turned back to her former home, determined to find more grey squirrels who would willingly leave the harsh Scarface and want to live in peace and tranquillity on Tolls Hill.

She scurried up a pine tree and ran quickly along the length of its branches and leapt gracefully through the air and on to the next tree. Suddenly in front of her she saw two large grey squirrels, talking together. They had not yet noticed her, but she froze on the spot. Her fear paralysed her, she could neither move, nor cry out. She knew that she ought to pass casually by, but her legs would not carry her. She heard further sounds to her side. From the corner of her eye she saw two more adult males approaching.

One of them, she saw with horror, had noticed her and was watching her with interest, whilst continuing to talk to his companion. Soon they were almost upon her.

'Hey. You there!'

Fern's tail twitched madly and her teeth chattered. Her whole body was rigid. The squirrel that had called to her was now standing directly in front of her, his eyes boring into hers.

'Are you deaf?' he demanded.

Still she could not reply. He turned to his companion. 'Well, Thistle, we've got a right one here. Lost her tongue, it seems.'

The other squirrel made no comment, but Fern saw that he was looking at her closely. Where had she seen him before? Then she sucked in her breath quickly. She remembered. He had been at her trial. Would he recognise her?

The other squirrel was still staring into her eyes, unnerving her. 'Don't you know that you are supposed to move over and let us pass?'

Fern felt a lump in her throat and was still unable to speak. The squirrel then lifted his paw and was about to cuff her when Thistle spoke.

'Let her be. We've got more important things to do than play with this youngster. Come on.'

He looked over to the other two squirrels who had been watching the confrontation with amusement.

'You two. Come with us.'

All four then left, leaving Fern feeling very relieved and amazed at her good fortune. For some time she sat on the branch unable to move. After a while the quivering stopped, and the thumping in her chest eased.

She was about to leave when Sunbeam appeared by her side. She looked surprised but pleased to see her friend again.

'Why didn't you stay with the others?'

He shrugged. 'I thought you might need some help.'

She nuzzled him gratefully and together they hurried off toward the centre of the island, determined to talk to some more friends and try to persuade them to leave, before it was too late.

Neither Fern nor Sunbeam had noticed the grey squirrel who had been listening to their every word. Thistle was too clever. He had sneaked back and hidden in a leafy branch just above them. He recognised Fern the moment he saw her and he knew that there must be something going on. She would not have returned to Grey Squirrel Island for nothing.

No, Thistle was going to get to the bottom of it. Stealthily he crept after them.

CHAPTER SIXTEEN

It's no good,' sighed Rowan, blood dripping from his mouth, 'we just can't do it.'

Owl was watching with concern. Redfox had sent him over to Group Two to see how they were getting on gnawing through the tree branches that were damming the river. He had arrived to find them exhausted, sore and disappointed.

'It's this last big branch. It's holding all the other branches in place, and we just can't bite through it. We're going to need some help.'

He lay down dejectedly, the blood from his mouth staining the fur on his chin and dripping into the water.

The Owl was worried. Time was running out and he had no time to think of an alternative plan. The success of the whole operation depended on the dam giving way. The only thing he could do was to go and tell Jasmine to start running, for surely the Grey Invaders would soon realise what was happening.

It was a sorry sight. The youngsters had been working so hard carrying away branches, lugging heavy stones and chewing and gnawing through branches and roots. He shook his head sadly and was about to fly off when there was a movement behind him, followed by a bump and then a curse. Nuthead appeared through the undergrowth, rubbing his head with his paw.

'Darned branches are far too low.'

Rowan looked at the rabbit and could not help but laugh. Nuthead looked around quickly and then turned to the Owl.

'What's the problem?'

The bird explained, and together they went over to the big branch and inspected it. It was thick, no doubt about that. It was easily twice as big as a squirrel. He could see the teeth marks where the red squirrels had been trying to gnaw through. He also saw the blood stains on the wood.

Nuthead shrugged. 'Not much we can do about that, is there?'

But the Owl was thinking. There was no way he was going to give up so easily.

'Nuthead,' he said urgently, 'could you go and get the other rabbits? Maybe they could gnaw through.'

'Hmmph,' said the rabbit, scratching his ear. Then he turned and ran back into the wood, calling 'Shan't be long,' as he went.

The Owl and Rowan exchanged glances, but said nothing. A young male squirrel came wearily over to the branch and began half-heartedly to claw at the bark. It was not long before his paws were bleeding badly.

'Leave it,' said the Owl, 'help is on its way.' The young squirrel nodded slowly and moved painfully away.

The Owl surveyed the scene before him. There was no doubt about it, they only had to move that one large branch and it would release all the branches behind it. Then the river would flow again. With a fierce determination the Owl stalked over to the root and began tugging it with his beak. Nothing. Then he jumped up and down on it. Still nothing. In frustration, he kicked it.

Rowan, watching nearby, could not help giggling at the bird's noble gesture. The Owl rose into the air, calling to Rowan. 'I'm going to report to Redfox.'

Rowan nodded. 'We'll have a rest....eh?'

The great bird soared over the oaks, chestnuts and pine trees. He was very annoyed about the big branch. Just then his keen eyes spotted a long trail of rabbits, headed by Nuthead. He immediately swooped down and spoke to Nuthead.

'Well done. Do you think it will work?' he asked.

The rabbit rubbed his paws over his ears and then over his face, and much to the Owl's surprise, lifted his lips back, revealing two rows of shiny white teeth.

'See these teeth?' he mumbled, still curling his lips, 'well, we've got a couple of dozen pairs here. Reckon we can soon get through that old branch.'

The Owl hooted in delight. 'Carry on then, and I'll tell Redfox everything is going according to plan.'

Nuthead nodded and bounded off, followed closely by the other rabbits. 'Come on, chaps,' he called. 'Let's go and help these young squirrels again.

'Reckon we can soon get through that old branch.'

The Owl watched them go, convinced they were actually marching. 'Nothing will surprise me about that rabbit,' he thought

'Here come *another* group,' gasped Chestnut as he raced out of the undergrowth. Just behind him came Fern, followed by a large group of curious grey squirrels. Redfox was full of praise.

'Well done, Fern. Well done. I think we should go now before the adults begin to suspect that something is wrong.'

'I can't give up yet,' she panted, her tail flicking excitedly. 'I've just seen a group of about twenty young females. I know some of them, and I'm sure they'll come if I speak to them.'

'No, Fern. Owl tells me they are nearly through the last main branch forming the dam. The river will be running soon and we can't risk your being stranded.'

Fern turned around determinedly. 'I must go back. I'll hurry, I promise.' And with a flash of her silver tail she was gone. Sunbeam watched her disappear.

'Come on, friend,' called Redfox, 'follow this squirrel here and he will take you to Tolls Hill.' Reluctantly Sunbeam obeyed, casting a sad glance in the direction Fern had taken.

Redfox was concerned. They had been travelling backwards and forwards to Tolls Hill and Grey Squirrel Island for such a long time. He was sure that almost half of the young greys had now left the island. There was a nagging worry that he could not dismiss. He could not understand why the adults had not found them. He had expected a fight, but there had been no sign of any of the guards. In fact, he felt that it was all too quiet.

Earlier there had been a constant noise coming from the island. Sounds of screeches and shouts. Now they could hear nothing except themselves as they returned from the hill.

'I don't like it,' he thought, 'I don't like it at all.'

There was a whoosh of air above and he looked up to see the Owl landing on a branch.

'Trouble!' he shouted. Cold fear crept over Redfox. 'Did you hear me? I said trouble.'

'Yes, Owl,' replied Redfox, 'what sort of trouble?'

The bird, looking around to ensure that he would not be overheard, moved closer to the squirrel.

'Young Fern is talking to a group of females, but there is an adult grey squirrel watching her from a nearby pine tree. I'm positive she doesn't know he is there.'

Greybeard stepped forward. 'It's time for me to go in,' he said firmly.

Redfox looked at this great squirrel and thought quickly. He knew they had no choice. He could think of no alternative so nodded in agreement.

'I agree. I would be too conspicuous with my red coat, whereas you might get away with it, being grey.'

He turned to the Owl. 'Please fly over and see how Group Two are doing so we can guess how long we have got.'

The Owl left quickly. The others waited patiently until he returned a few moments later. 'Not long now. The rabbits are nearly through.'

'Right then,' said Greybeard, 'which way do I go?'

'Follow me,' said the bird.

Redfox put his paw out to Greybeard. 'Good luck,' he murmured. Without a word Greybeard dashed off in pursuit of the Owl.

There was much discussion. Some wanted to go, others were not so sure. Fern was becoming increasingly worried. She knew there was little time left, but these squirrels would not make up their minds.

'Please,' she pleaded, 'we must go now, or it will be too late.'

'But it's quite nice here.'

'Yes, but Scarface is a tyrant.'

'But we don't like red squirrels.'

'Have you ever met one?'

'No, but.....'

'Then how can you say that you don't like them?'

'But the guards said.....'

'But what do *you* think?'

'I don't know. What do you think?'

'It might be exciting.'

'But it's quite nice here.'

Fern sighed. She would have to go, take those who would follow and leave the rest.

At that moment there was a terrible noise behind her. There was a streak of grey, followed by another, then a terrible shriek. They all watched in amazement. There on the ground were two of the largest grey squirrels they had ever seen. They were clawing and biting each other viciously.

'It's Thistle,' squealed one of the females.

'And Greybeard,' whispered Fern.

The two squirrels were rolling over and over, their eyes blazing and their teeth glistening with saliva and blood. They fell apart for a moment, and Greybeard shouted to Fern.

'Run, now!'

Thistle, about to jump on his opponent, paused in surprise.

'Who are you?' he demanded.

'I am Greybeard.'

Thistle gasped. He had been standing on his hind legs in the attack position. Now he dropped slowly on to all fours, much to Greybeard's surprise.

'Greybeard? It's not possible!'

'It is possible. I'm living proof.'

To Greybeard's further surprise, the squirrel curled his tail over his back and crouched low on the ground.

'I am honoured to meet you, sir. I apologise for my aggression. You took me somewhat by surprise.'

Greybeard was bemused. 'Why have you been watching Fern?'

Thistle sat down. 'By Fern, I assume you mean that young grey over there. I have been following her for a long time, listening to what she has to say.'

'I had no idea,' cried Fern.

'It's alright, Fern,' said Greybeard. 'Now tell me, what are you going to do?'

'I want to come with you,' declared Thistle.

There were gasps and exclamations from the female group.

'How do I know we can trust you?'

'Look at it logically,' he replied. 'If I was going to stop you, I could have alerted the other guards ages ago.'

'That's true,' said Greybeard thoughtfully. The two looked at each other with interest. The Owl, who had been watching and listening, suddenly let out a loud squawk.

'The guards are coming. The guards are coming.'

Greybeard looked at Thistle in alarm. 'So you were lying. You did call the guards.'

Thistle shook his head quickly. 'No, I promise you I did not. They must have heard us fighting.'

Greybeard considered this. Thistle looked genuinely alarmed. Panic had broken out amongst the females.

'I'm going to have to believe you, Thistle. Quickly,' yelled Greybeard, 'you've got to go *now*.'

'Follow me,' called Fern. 'Run! Run!'

Several of the females followed Fern into the woods.

'I'll delay them,' said Thistle.

Greybeard paused. 'No. Come with us. Help me defend them in case we get attacked from behind.'

Together they raced away, following Fern's group. There was still a large group left undecided.

'If Thistle is going, then so am I.'

'Me too.'

'And me.'

Finally all of them were tearing through the woods. They were all racing along, purposely keeping to the track on the ground so that their pursuers would be confused by the smell.

'The trouble is,' panted Thistle, 'there are so many of us they will hear the commotion.'

'Don't talk. Just run.'

Suddenly there was a loud shriek from far behind, followed by several angry screeches.

'Stop them!'

'Call the guards. Stop the runaways.'

Then the whole island seemed to come alive. There were screams and yells, and shouts from everywhere. The females were terrified but they kept running. On and on they went, brambles snatching at their faces and tails, thorns tearing into their sides. They stumbled and moaned but did their best to keep up. There was a burst of grey from the side and suddenly another squirrel was running alongside Greybeard and Thistle.

'Nettle!' wheezed Thistle.

'Can I join you?' he asked of Greybeard as they ran. Greybeard turned his head briefly to look at the tailless squirrel.

'Did they do that?' he asked. Nettle nodded. 'Then join us,' said Greybeard.

The pursuers were getting closer; they could hear the sounds of pounding feet behind. Ahead of them, at the end of the track, Greybeard could see Redfox and the others, waiting. Redfox was shouting, but they could hardly hear him.

'I...can't...hear...you,' gasped Greybeard.

'The river,' Redfox yelled. 'Run. *Run.*'

Greybeard understood. The dam had broken, and the river was coming. He tried to ignore the pain in his body, and awful wrenching in his chest. He blinked rapidly and tried to clear his vision, which had misted over. Where was Redfox now? He couldn't see him. He must keep running. Then he felt a sharp pain in his side, as if a gigantic thorn had pierced his flesh. He longed to stop and rest. 'Just a little further,' he thought desperately.

There were squeals of fright behind him.

'They're coming. They're going to catch us.'

With an almighty effort, Greybeard shouted to the others. 'No they won't, not if you're quick. Run to the red squirrels ahead. Run as fast as you can.'

He could hear the sound of running water. He remembered the size of the dam. It was so big it must have held a tremendous amount of water. It would race down the river bed in a torrent and wash them all away. Was it too late? The thorn in his side was piercing him. It was excruciating.

He paused for a split second to catch his breath. The pain in his chest was unbearable. Thistle paused too.

'Go on,' urged Greybeard.

He began to run again. Thistle was ahead of him now. He was last. Would they make it?

Suddenly there was a howl and he was bowled over. Sharp claws dug into his skin and a harsh voice screeched in his ear.

'I've got you now, you traitor!'

Scarface! With an almighty effort Greybeard twisted and curled until Scarface fell from his back. He knew this was his one chance and he had to take it. Before Scarface could get up Greybeard was on him, sinking his teeth into his throat.

Scarface rolled and twisted but he could not break Greybeard's grip. The teeth were sinking deeper. Scarface howled. With every last ounce of strength Greybeard kicked at Scarface with his strong back legs. Scarface moaned, and was still.

Then he heard the shouts of Redfox and the others and tried to get up. The pain in his chest was too much. He saw the ground coming up to meet him and felt his nose being crushed in the damp earth. He heard the squeals behind him and heard too the sound of the rushing water. Then everything went black. Then the noises faded away. Then nothing.

The squirrels watched as the bodies of Greybeard and Scarface were carried away by the torrent of water. Redfox herded the terrified females away from the water. The river came like a torrential storm, crashing and roaring, uprooting everything in its path.

Nettle and Thistle watched silently as Scarface, brought round by the coldness of the water, struggled and cried and then disappeared beneath the surface. They looked sadly at the grey squirrels opposite, frightened and confused. Quietly and efficiently Redfox led the group away, back towards Tolls Hill, and safety.

In a tree overhead, the Owl sobbed at the loss of his friend.

CHAPTER SEVENTEEN

It was a glorious sunny day on Tolls Hill. The early morning dew still glistened on the cobwebs and bees buzzed merrily over the clover. There was a gentle, cool breeze in the air.

At the bottom of the hill, a group of rabbits chattered together, and a stoat, passing by, hardly gave them a second glance. Every now and then a red streak could be seen, followed by a silver streak. There was much laughter and both red and grey youngsters tumbled and played in the long grass.

In the tree-tops sat a silent group of squirrels, watching the scenes below. Fern sighed, and nuzzled against Rowan. He licked her ear affectionately. He caught his mother's eye and she twitched her whiskers at him. The new drey was ready now; he and Fern would shortly be moving into it. The thought of leaving his home drey filled him with fear and excitement, but he was looking forward to his new life with Fern. After all, Jasmine would only be a few trees away.

Amber smiled. It was good. Fern and Rowan would take over from her and Greybeard, showing the squirrel world that reds and greys could live happily together.

'Greybeard would be so proud,' she sighed. The others nodded silently. Amber seemed to want to talk about him, so they listened.

'He was too old, you know, for such antics. But he was determined to fight Scarface, to repay his debt to the red squirrels.'

Jasmine moved to her side and touched noses with her.

'Now that Rowan is moving, you are welcome to share my drey,' she whispered.

Amber smiled sadly. 'You, Jasmine, have been a wonderful friend. We have been through so much together over the years. I look down below now and wonder how we ever did it.'

She turned to the others, her eyes misty. 'There is nothing for me without Greybeard. I know that Tolls Hill will be the start of something wonderful. I hope there will never again be wars between squirrels, be they red or grey.'

With that, she edged out of the drey and began to descend the tree. She paused briefly.

'I shall not see you again, but do not be sad. I have had a good life and for many summers Greybeard and I were happy. I am going now to join Greybeard.'

The others watched as she went. They saw her go down the hill, look around once, look up at the sky, and then determinedly enter the dark wood.

'I had a dream last night,' Rowan told Fern. 'It was about a giant acorn. Inside there were mountains of sweet-chestnuts and pine cones, and there was a waterfall of sparkling water, and red and grey squirrels played and ate there, and it was a beautiful place.'

'It sounds lovely,' whispered Fern.

'Yes, it was,' replied Rowan thoughtfully, remembering that he had had a similar dream…such a long time ago.

They nuzzled each other tenderly.

'Rowan?'

'Mmmm?'

'They won't ever come back, will they?'

'The Grey Invaders? No, they'll never come back.'

'How can you be sure?'

'Because the river now surrounds the island again, and it runs so fast no squirrel could ever swim it.'

'So....I could never go back?'

Rowan hesitated. 'Would you want to?'

Fern thought for a moment. 'No, I wouldn't. I have never been so happy as I am here.'

'Owl says that there has been no more fighting over there.'

'I'm glad,' she murmured as she curled up and began to doze.

Rowan looked up at the rising sun, and drank in the glorious colours all around him and smelt the sweet smell of the morning. He had much to thank Amber and Greybeard for, and he vowed that he would never forget them.

Leaving Fern silently, he crept to the uppermost branches of the home tree and looked out towards Squirrel Island.

'Live in peace now,' he whispered. There was a movement on the next tree and there sat Jasmine. She, too, was looking over to the island.

'Is it finally over?' he called softly to her. She looked from the island to her son and back again.

'Yes,' she murmured. 'Yes. It's finally over.'